RANGER REDEMPTION

TEXAS RANGER HEROES

LYNN SHANNON

This novel is dedicated to my parents. You taught integrity, perseverance, and a strong work ethic. Everything I've accomplished has grown from the seeds you planted. I love you.

Love is patient, love is kind. It does not envy, it does not boast, it is not proud. It does not dishonor others, it is not self-seeking, it is not easily angered, it keeps no record of wrongs. Love does not delight in evil but rejoices with the truth.

1 CORINTHIANS 13: 4-6

ONE

Luke's heart rate spiked as he steered his Texas Ranger-issued Suburban near the broken guardrail. Its jagged edges yawned toward the steep drop-off, and a foreboding cloud of smoke rose from the ravine. Acrid scents of burning oil and melted plastic overtook those of the wild-flowers and grass. He radioed into dispatch. Backup was less than five minutes out. Judging from the plumes of smoke, any survivors in the vehicle below didn't have that much time left.

The woman who'd waved him down ran up when he opened his door. "Thank goodness you're here. I have my daughter in the car—"

"Were you injured in the accident? Anyone in your vehicle hurt?"

"No." She swallowed hard. "I wasn't involved. I was driving past and saw the break in the guardrail."

"Good, then get in your truck and move half a mile down the road." On the off chance the car in the ravine exploded, he didn't want her anywhere nearby. "A sheriff's deputy will come find you."

Leaving the turret lights flashing, he pulled open the tailgate and snatched the first aid kit tucked between the crime-scene kit and the rifle. He also grabbed the fire extinguisher.

Lord, please don't let me be too late. Give me the strength to help.

He raced to the road's edge.

Below in the ravine, a sedan—or what Luke thought had once been a sedan—was now a hunk of twisted metal. Glass littered the rocks. Crushed vegetation indicated the vehicle hadn't just gone over the edge of the drop-off from the winding country road; it had rolled several times before landing upside down. Flames shot out of the front end.

Luke's chest squeezed tight. He hated fires.

He tore down the slope, smoke blowing in his face and obscuring his vision. His cowboy boots skidded along the gravel, and Luke slipped landing on his rear. The first aid kit jabbed him in the back. His hand, slick with sweat, nearly lost its grip on the fire extinguisher.

He righted himself and kept going. Smoke burned his lungs. His eyes watered. Luke held his breath, his pulse pounding in his ears.

The wind shifted. He took several deep breaths of fresh air and tasted ash on his tongue. Wiping his eyes with his sleeve, he closed the last few feet with long strides. Heat from the fire seared him. He yanked the pin from the fire extinguisher and unloaded it.

Seconds. Precious seconds. But it might slow the fire down enough to get people out. In the distance, sirens blared. Tossing the empty fire extinguisher aside, he lunged for the opening created by the broken passenger-side window. A woman hung upside down in the driver's seat. Blood ran from her head, coating the side of her face and her blonde hair streaked with gray. She was unconscious.

Luke sucked in a sharp breath. "Oh, no."

It was his ex-fiancée's aunt, June. Megan could not lose the woman who'd raised her. Not like this. A stronger sense of urgency welled in his chest. He scanned the interior of the car. June was the only occupant. Ignoring the glass scattered along the roof, he drew closer. She moaned and her eyes fluttered.

"June, can you hear me?" He felt along her neck. The bones seemed intact. Still, moving her could be dangerous—it could kill her—but he didn't have a choice. The fire wasn't completely out and he smelled gas fumes. The car could be engulfed in a flash.

"No brakes," she muttered.

"Let's get you out of here." He braced June with his arm and pulled a knife from his boot. He sliced through the seat belt. She fell onto him and moaned again. Heat warmed his back. A glance proved the temporary reprieve was over. The flames were back. And growing.

"This will hurt," Luke warned. He wriggled out, pulling June with him. Glass scratched his hands and tore at his pants. June's gaze met his and she stiffened.

She clutched his arm. Her mouth moved, her eyes pleading and desperate.

Sweat beaded on his forehead. "Almost there—"

Her grip tightened, nails cutting into his skin. "Megan," she whispered.

It was almost a prayer, and Luke's heart stuttered.

"Find Megan. D-D-Dan—" June's eyes rolled back in her head as her body shook violently Luke looked up. Medics stood at the road's edge.

He gathered June in his arms and ran.

TWO

The hospital smelled like a mixture of bleach and disease. Almost midnight and the normal hustle and bustle was quiet, the lights dimmed to accommodate sleeping patients. Megan perched on the edge of the visitor's chair and held her aunt's hand like it was made of spun glass. June's face was bruised, her petite body swallowed up by the stiff sheets. Wires, tubes, and machines crowded the space around the bed.

"June, you have to wake up and get better." A tear slipped down Megan's cheek.

Her parents were dead and her only brother was in prison. Her aunt was all she had left. She squeezed her eyes shut, the embedded urge to pray bubbling up, but she squelched it. Megan and God hadn't been on speaking terms for a while.

"Miss, I'm sorry, but visiting hours are over."

Megan opened her eyes to find a nurse standing at the bedside. The woman offered her a sympathetic smile.

"You can come back tomorrow morning. ICU patients are allowed brief visits every hour."

"And—" She swallowed past the lump. "If something happens during the night?"

"We'll call you." The nurse hung a new IV bag. "Your aunt is in critical condition, but she's stable."

Megan clung to the word stable. Any other alternative was too painful to consider. She bent and gently kissed her aunt's cheek.

"I'll be back tomorrow," she whispered. "I love you."

She retrieved her purse and jacket from the chair and, on wooden legs, walked out of the room. Luke was leaning against the wall on the opposite side of the hall and straightened when he spotted her. It'd been three years since they'd last seen each other, and a world of hurt separated them, but her heart still skipped a beat when his gaze met hers. The crooked scar at the corner of his mouth and the slight bulge along the bridge of his nose—testaments to his troubled youth—were more evident by the short haircut and five o'clock shadow gracing his jaw. Mud spattered the legs of his khakis and cowboy boots.

"How is she?"

"She's in a coma." Her chin trembled, and she blinked rapidly to fight back a fresh wave of tears. "They don't know if she's going to make it."

"She'll make it, Megs." Luke edged closer until he was standing in front of her. "Remember when June was breaking Remnant? Meanest horse in the county. No one else would touch him."

"It took June weeks to even get close to him." The corners of her mouth lifted slightly at the memory, even as she swiped at the dampness on her cheeks. "Everyone kept telling her it was useless, but she refused to give up."

"Exactly. And she won't give up this time either."

She sucked in a deep breath. The temptation to take one step, lay her head against his chest, and cry a mountain of tears in his strong arms was compelling. Luke wasn't just her ex-fiancé. Until their breakup, he'd also been her best friend and confidant. She lifted her gaze. A fresh scratch ran along his neck and disappeared into the collar of his wrinkled shirt.

"Thank you, Luke. For saving June. The doctor said another few minutes and—"

She would've died.

The words clogged her throat. He raised his hand as if to touch her arm but stopped halfway and dropped it. The fluorescent light caught on the Texas Ranger badge pinned to his chest. She willed herself to step away. Their relationship was like a shattered mirror, damaged and altered beyond repair. June's accident, and Luke's heroic actions, didn't change that.

He shoved his hands in his pockets. "Megs, we need to talk."

Her gaze darted to the state trooper standing outside of June's room and she nodded. Avoiding this conversation wasn't an option. She couldn't make decisions without understanding exactly what was happening.

He led her to an empty break room. An ancient fridge in the corner hummed. Plastic chairs were scattered around a scratched table, and a comedy show played silently on the television in the corner.

She set her jacket and purse on the table. "What do you know about my aunt's accident?"

Luke stepped over to the coffee machine and poured the dark brew into two Styrofoam cups. He handed one to her and she took it, careful not to let their fingers brush.

"Why don't you sit down?" He jerked his chin at a chair. "It's been a long night."

"I'm okay. Just tell me."

"She was on old Kerrville Road and went off the embankment along a sharp curve."

Megan flinched. The road was notoriously dangerous. What was her aunt doing there? And did it have anything to do with the voice mail she'd left this afternoon on Megan's phone? She took a sip of coffee, and it swirled like battery acid in her stomach.

"June was conscious when I pulled her from the car," Luke continued. "She muttered something about her brakes not working. I found evidence at the scene to support her claim. There were no skid marks and the rocks along the road's edge were scraped away. Blue paint, a color consistent with June's vehicle, was also found near the scrapes. I think she banged the car into the rocks lining the road in an effort to slow down. Had she been having trouble with her car?"

"No." The room tilted slightly as her worst fears were realized. "Are you suggesting her brakes were tampered with? That someone attempted to kill her?"

"I don't know for sure. I've had the car towed to the evidence shed and a forensic team will be out first thing in the morning." His jaw tightened. "But if we were taking bets, my guess is yes."

Megan's legs jellied. She gripped the back of a chair for support, her knuckles turning white with the effort.

"Can you think of any reason why someone would hurt June?" Luke asked.

She closed her eyes, struggling with how to answer that question. June was a private investigator, and she'd made quite a few people mad over the years, but it seemed ridiculous to consider this could all be a coincidence. Her aunt's instructions in the voice mail had been clear. Come home. Tell no one. Trust no one. Goose bumps pebbled her arms.

What should she do?

Lying went against her instincts and her morals, but she'd trusted Luke before and her brother had ended up in prison as a result. Even if she told him the truth now, would he believe her?

"Megs, there's something else you should know." Luke's boots tapped against the floor and she felt, rather than saw, him come up next to her. "Your aunt begged me to find you. I think she was trying to tell me you were in danger."

She sucked in a sharp breath and faced him. "She told you that?"

He nodded. "If someone tried to kill June, the perpetrator might make a second attempt once news she survived gets out. I can't protect you or her from something I don't understand. Whatever it is, you need to tell me."

She wrapped her arms around herself. None of her choices were great, but she wouldn't put her aunt's life at risk.

"It's about Wade, Luke." She lifted her gaze to look him in the eyes. "June found proof of his innocence. That's why someone tried to kill her."

It took every ounce of Luke's law enforcement training to keep his expression impassive, but his heart thundered like a stampede of horses. Overhead, the hospital speaker came on, announcing a Code Blue. Megan's eyes widened and she froze.

He reacted instinctively, reaching out to grasp her arm. "It's not June's room. It's the one next to hers."

"You're sure?"

The naked terror and pain on her face made his heart ache. Megan had lost her parents in a car wreck. June's accident—horrible in its own right—had to be a cruel reminder.

"I'm positive, Megs. It's not for her."

He squeezed her arm gently. The desire to embrace her clawed at him, and memories he'd shoved into the far recesses of his mind rose like a tidal wave. She'd been his first love, the woman he'd thought he would spend his life with. She'd also broken his heart.

He gave himself a mental shake. Their relationship,

and its fallout, was in the past. It didn't matter. Luke wouldn't *allow* it to matter. He had a job to do.

He released her and took a step back. "Megs, what makes you think June's accident has anything to do with Wade?"

She drew her spine up and adjusted her blouse. Tear tracks lined her cheeks and the faint smattering of freckles along her nose stood out against her pale skin, but her mouth hardened.

"June claimed to have found evidence of Wade's innocence. She told me about it right before her accident."

He stared at her. How was that possible? Wade had confessed to murdering his friend, Franny Dickerson, in a jealous rage. The act had been fueled not just by unrequited feelings but also with alcohol.

Megan seemed to hear his question before he could ask it because she held up a finger. "Hold on."

She reached for her purse. Her hair, the color of hay dried in the sun, fell over her forehead. She shoved it out of the way. The scent of her shampoo wafted his direction. Honeysuckle. The flower was popular in Texas, and every time he caught its fragrance, he thought of her.

Megan pulled out her cell phone. "June called me this afternoon, but I was in a trial and couldn't answer. I'd forgotten all about it until I was driving here from Houston. When I checked, I saw she'd left me a voice mail."

She pushed something on the phone's screen and turned up the volume. June's voice spilled from the speaker.

Megs, our prayers have been answered. I've found evidence that proves Wade is innocent. You need to come home now, but quietly. No one can know. We can't trust anyone. Call me when you get this.

The muscles in Luke's shoulders stiffened. "What time was that call?"

"Four fifteen."

"Your aunt's accident happened around four thirty." His mind raced as he tried to make sense of the information. "Did she call you again?"

Megan shook her head. "Was there anything in the car? A file folder, maybe?"

They'd conducted a search of the vehicle and the ravine to secure possible evidence and hadn't found much.

"We recovered her cell phone, but it was smashed. Her credit cards and driver's license were in the case." He ran a hand through his hair. "How is it possible she found evidence of Wade's innocence? He confessed to Franny's murder."

"Under duress," she snapped.

"Are you suggesting Sheriff Franklin coerced him?"

"No, but I think the sheriff was under a lot of pressure to solve the case. Some things may have been overlooked."

"Like what?"

She speared him with a look. "You know as well as I do that Wade wasn't acting right in the days after the murder. I think he saw something the night Franny was killed and he's too scared to say what it was."

"If that's true, then he would have told the sheriff. He wouldn't have confessed to the murder."

She crossed her arms over her chest. "If my aunt didn't know who to trust, how would Wade?"

The question socked him like a punch to the gut. In the years since her brother's conviction, Luke had reasoned Wade's nervous behavior was attributed to guilt.

"You're telling me Wade confessed to Franny's murder because someone threatened him?"

"Not him. I think someone could've been threatening to harm June or me. There's nothing Wade wouldn't have done to protect us." Megan scowled. "If you had just *talked* to him, convinced him to tell you the truth, we wouldn't be in this mess now."

"Megs, there are things about your brother—"

"What? That he was partying? Drinking? He'd gotten in trouble for some barroom brawls." The color in her cheeks deepened. "I already know, Luke. June came clean after his confession. Too bad neither of you thought to tell me before it was too late."

Her tone was caustic. He opened his mouth, but she cut him off with a slice of her hand through the air. "Don't. There's nothing you can say to fix it now."

He gritted his teeth and wrestled with his temper. What was the point? She was right. They were too far gone for explanations. Not that she'd given him the chance—ever—to give one.

"Fighting grown men in a bar or drinking too much is a far cry from murdering a woman in cold blood." She jutted up her chin. "I don't believe Wade is capable of it, and the only reason he confessed is because he was forced to."

"How do you know all of this? Has Wade told you?"

"My aunt spent some time looking into the case after his arrest. We managed to put a couple of things together." Her shoulders slumped. "Wade refuses to talk about it. He insists June and I both leave it alone."

Megan was a criminal defense attorney. If Wade refused her help, there were only two explanations. Either he was guilty or he was trying to protect her. June's recent attack coupled with the voice mail gave serious weight to the latter. A cold, insidious finger of self-doubt crept across Luke's heart like barbed wire. He closed his eyes. *God, did I help put an innocent man in jail?*

The concept made his stomach roll. When Megan had come to him and shared that Wade had been in the cabin with Franny on the night of her murder, Luke had taken the information straight to the sheriff. His decision led to chain of events affecting all of them. Wade was arrested and convicted. Megan broke off their engagement. Luke felt the responsibility of his choices resting on his shoulders, weighted down by the ranger badge and his own personal code of conduct.

"Do you have any idea what the evidence June found might be?"

"No. I didn't even know June was investigating until I heard the voice mail." Megan stared down at the table. "If the evidence wasn't with her, then where is it?"

"The vehicle caught fire. It's possible the evidence was destroyed." He blew out a breath. "The forensic unit will go over the car with a fine-tooth comb, but I'll tell them to keep an eye out anyway. I'll also put out feelers to see if June was asking questions around town about Franny's murder."

Megan opened her mouth, and he held up a hand.

"Hold on, I want to be clear. I'm not convinced Wade is innocent, but I'm also not going to ignore what's right in front of me. If there is any way June's accident is connected to Franny's murder, then it's a thread I have to pull."

Her lips flattened into a thin line, but she nodded. "Visiting hours are over, so I won't be able to see June until tomorrow morning. I'll stay at the house tonight."

Luke caught his objection moments before it left his mouth. As a law enforcement officer, he needed a warrant or permission from June to search her house. Megan didn't. She only needed lawful entry, which she had, thanks to her spare key. No doubt the brilliant woman was five steps ahead of him and had already figured that out. He couldn't help her search for the evidence, but he could provide protection.

"I'll follow you home and make sure you get there okay."

Megan nodded, her hair caressing her cheeks, before turning to collect her jacket and purse. He watched her, a mix of emotions churning inside him. She'd shown up only two hours ago, and yet her reappearance in his life had imploded everything Luke thought he knew.

THREE

His hand tightened around the syringe filled with enough barbiturates to kill a horse.

He adjusted the doctor's surgical mask over the lower half of his face and peeked out from inside the supply closet. The scrubs he'd stolen from the back of a truck in the parking lot smelled like musky cologne and his stomach revolted. A trooper stood guard outside June's hospital room. Even dressed in disguise, there was no way he could slip by unnoticed and finish the job.

A string of curse words ran through his head. June should be dead. That road was rarely used. What were the chances a good Samaritan would see the wreck and call it in?

The door leading to the break room opened, and Megan appeared followed by Luke. Her chin was high, and there was a determined march to her step. His teeth ground together. The ranger was an aggravation, but one he could manage. He had connections, and he knew the pressure points. Wade's sister, on the other hand, was a wild card and far too much like her aunt. He should have gotten rid of the Hunt family a long time ago.

He took a deep breath to settle his nerves. There was no reason to panic. Not yet. Things hadn't gone as planned, but they hadn't gone badly either. June was in a coma. She couldn't tell them anything. Luke suspected foul play, but with the car in such bad shape, it was possible they would never find proof.

Still, he needed to calculate his next moves carefully. He ducked behind the door as Megan and Luke passed by the room. His gaze narrowed into slits. Little did she know, but Megan was a dead woman walking. So was her entire family. One by one, he would smash them into oblivion.

The couple disappeared around the corner. His phone vibrated. He released the syringe and flexed his fingers before unhooking the phone from his belt.

"It's about time you return my call."

"Things are busy down here and I can't disappear any time I want. But don't worry, I have the information you need. Let's meet."

They arranged a time and place before he hung up. Checking to make sure the coast was clear, he slipped from the supply closet. The drive wasn't long, but it would be enough to plan. To figure out exactly how he would mop this mess up.

Megan wasn't the only loose end he needed to tie off.

FOUR

Luke rubbed his chilled hands together before shoving them in his jacket pockets. The porch swing rocked and trees on the outer edge of June's yard rustled with the wind. Lights inside the house glowed. June had run her private investigation business out of her home, and it seemed Megan was focusing on the office first.

Headlights made their way down the street. Two quick flashes bounced off the rearview mirror, and Luke relaxed against the seat. A Medina County Sheriff's patrol vehicle pulled up next to his, Lieutenant Brent Granger behind the wheel.

Motion detection lights attached to the house lit up Brent's face. A dark beard covered his jaw, an offset to the boyish cheeks plaguing him since grade school. His head was shaved—in solidarity with his mother who was undergoing chemo treatments—and Brent's shoulders bunched up to his ears as he crossed the distance between the two vehicles. When he opened the passenger-side door, a gust of icy wind scented with french fries slipped in.

Brent hefted his weight into Luke's truck, the movement fluid despite the bulk of his duty belt and bulletproof vest. "Holy moly, it's freezing out here."

"You doing the night shift again?" Luke asked, bumping up the heat to ward off the chill. "I thought those days were behind you."

Brent had been with the sheriff's department for almost a decade. As a lieutenant, he didn't normally do patrol.

"Watson has a new baby. I'm picking up some of his shifts so he can help out his wife." He handed Luke a large takeaway mug and a bag from a fast food place. "I heard about June's accident from Sheriff Franklin when I showed up for my shift. He said you were worried about it being foul play and that Megan might be in danger."

Luke set the coffee in a cup holder and fished fries from the bag. He quickly ran through his conversation with Megan, including her suspicion that June's accident was connected to Franny's murder.

Brent whistled. "Wow. No wonder the sheriff and the chief deputy were huddling in his office tonight."

Dan Carter, currently the chief deputy, had been the lead investigator on Franny's murder case. Brent had assisted.

"How do you think Dan handled the investigation?" Luke asked.

"There was a lot of pressure to solve Franny's

murder. Megan isn't wrong about that, but everything Wade told us lined up."

"I figured as much."

"You did nothing wrong, Luke." He twisted in the seat to face him. "Wade was in love with Franny and angry because she didn't feel the same way. It was an argument fueled by drinking that went sideways. You can't let your feelings for Megan interfere with the investigation."

"I'm not." He jerked the bag of food away. "I have my eyes wide open."

Brent's jaw tightened.

Luke took a deep breath, realizing that his tone was more hostile than necessary. His friend's warning wasn't unjustified. As much as he hated to admit it, Luke couldn't completely divest himself of his emotions when it came to Megan.

He took another deep breath. "I don't intend to work this case by myself. I have a plan."

"Okay." Brent paused. "Just...tread lightly. The Dickersons will be upset if you reopen Franny's case. They won't be the only ones."

"I know. One thing at a time. Let's see what the forensic unit finds when they examine June's vehicle."

"Yeah, okay." Brent reached for the door handle. "I better get back on patrol. I'm on till six so let me know if you need anything."

"Hey, before you go, how's your mom doing?"

"She's not bouncing back from the chemo like she did

with the first round of cancer, but she keeps fighting. Thanks for sending over the flowers. She loved them."

"Anything I can do, let me know. And Brent, I appreciate the coffee and the advice."

"Anytime."

Brent strolled back to his vehicle, and his taillights faded into the night. Luke's gaze drifted back to June's house. The living room lights were still on. Megan was being thorough, and for the hundredth time that night, Luke wasn't sure what outcome he was hoping for.

Early-morning sunlight creeped across the countertop. The scent of fresh coffee filled the kitchen, and Megan breathed it in, hoping for a jolt of caffeine by smell alone. The metallic toaster morphed her reflection, but nothing could hide the dark circles under her eyes. She'd been up most of the night searching for the evidence.

Archimedes, her aunt's cat, twined around her legs. He let out a meow.

"Yes, yes. I suppose the first order of business is you." She fed him, and the tabby cat attacked the bowl with gusto. Megan laughed. "I fed you last night. You can't be that hungry."

The coffee finished dripping, and she poured a cup. An open bag of jelly beans she'd discovered hidden in her aunt's office sat on the counter and she popped a couple in her mouth, chasing them with a sip of the strong dark brew. The cat, now finished with his food, slanted a look her way.

"Don't judge me. I'm exhausted."

She unearthed a portable mug from the cabinet and filled it with coffee. When she stepped outside, a slap of sharp cold bit her cheeks. The sun peeked over the horizon. Tendrils of light sparkled on the morning dew, and the grass shimmered like diamonds.

Luke leaned against his vehicle, texting something on his phone. His gaze lifted to meet hers and his lips tipped at the corners. "Morning."

"Good morning." She handed him the travel mug.

His smile grew wider, and her traitorous heart skipped a beat. She shifted her gaze to the house and the barn beyond. She was here to prove Wade's innocence and get June well, not to deal with the lingering feelings from her broken relationship with Luke.

He took a long sip of the coffee. When he lowered the mug, his expression grew serious. "Any news on June this morning?"

"Still in a coma. The doctor didn't say much."

She felt pulled in multiple directions. A large part of her wanted to be at the hospital, holding June's hand, but her aunt would be the first to say Megan needed to focus on proving Wade's innocence.

"They have to be cautious," Luke said softly. "If she hasn't worsened, it's a win."

She nodded. "I keep reminding myself of that."

"I don't suppose you've had any luck on your search."

"Not yet, but I still have to go through my aunt's bedroom."

She'd saved it for last. Although it was a necessary step and one her aunt would understand, it was an invasion of June's privacy. Megan had hoped the evidence would be somewhere else in the house.

She chewed on the inside of her cheek. "Would you like breakfast?"

Say no, say no, say no. The last thing she wanted to do was break bread with the man who'd hurt her so deeply, but Luke had slept in his vehicle outside last night, protecting her. The manners her mother instilled in her wouldn't allow Megan to refuse him basic hospitality.

Her mixed emotions must have shown in her expression because he frowned and said, "No, I'll get breakfast at my place, thanks."

"Okay."

He gestured toward the barn. "I took care of Cinnamon this morning. She's out in the pasture and her stall is clean."

She stiffened. "You didn't have to do that."

The words came out snappy and harsh. What was wrong with her?

He scratched his chin. "It was only one horse, Megs. It's not a big deal."

With a jolt, her brain caught up with her emotions. After Wade's conviction, June had sold all their other horses, including Megan's. It was a reasonable choice—it was a lot to keep up with on her own—but losing Fiona, her gentle quarter horse, still stung. Another thing her family had lost, part of the fallout she blamed on Luke.

He took another drink of coffee. "Hank will come by in half an hour to watch over things while I go home and grab a fresh change of clothes."

Luke's stepfather was a man of few words and the ones he spoke were often gruff, but he was as steady as an old oak tree. He'd married Nancy, Luke's mother, and they'd moved to Cardin ten years ago. Luke had followed after college.

"Do you think that's necessary?" she asked. "I'm sure Hank has better things to do."

"Naw, gives him an excuse to get away from tilling Mom's new garden. You're helping him out. Besides, I'm not taking any chances. You shouldn't either. When you go back inside, lock the door behind you."

"I will."

Megan walked back to the house. The warmth inside embraced her and her cheeks tingled. She stripped off her boots and jacket. Her aunt's cat was nestled on the couch. He blinked his bicolored eyes at her.

"Where would June have hidden the evidence, Archimedes?" She stroked his fur, and he purred. "You're no help."

Megan poured a fresh cup of coffee and took it to June's bedroom. Sunlight drifted through the pale-blue curtains. The checkered comforter was tucked under the pillows, and it smelled of furniture polish and lavender. A worn Bible rested on the nightstand. Next to it, a framed photograph caught her eye and twisted her heart until it hurt to breathe.

It'd been taken the day of her brother's high school graduation. Wade, standing between her and June, had an arm slung around each woman. His cap was askew on his head, the wind billowing his gown around his knees. They were all caught midlaugh, blissfully unaware that in in few short years, Wade would be convicted of murder and their entire lives would be altered forever.

Megan squared her shoulders. Enough. It was time to get to work.

The evidence had to be here, and she would find it.

Luke's lower back ached from sitting in his vehicle all night, and his eyes felt gritty. Keeping watch over June's house—and Megan—had been necessary, but it hadn't done his body any favors. He buttoned up a fresh shirt and pointedly refused to look at the bed. There wasn't time for a catnap.

He tucked his Sig P226 into its holster and adjusted the sports coat to cover it before picking up the knife from his nightstand. Luke rubbed the ornate pearl handle. It'd been a gift from June when he first learned of his acceptance into the academy. A foreshadowing, or perhaps God's intervention, the same knife had cut her free from the car yesterday. Sending up a quick prayer for June's recovery, Luke tucked the knife into his boot.

His cell phone vibrated against the dresser top, and he scooped it up, glancing at the caller ID.

His father. Again.

Luke's finger hovered over the phone before he hit the reject button. Patrick Tatum had moved to town six months ago, asking for grace and seeking to reconnect. Forgiveness had been easy to give. Sitting in anger over his father's addiction and subsequent abandonment had been eating Luke alive, and for his own sake, he'd forgiven Patrick a long time ago. But forming a relationship with his father was a different matter. The last attempt, fifteen years ago, had ended in heartache.

The cold snaked under his jacket as he walked between his house and the main one. Clouds, thick with rain, hung on the horizon. Voices filtered out from the kitchen and the heavenly scent of biscuits wafted into the mudroom. Luke shrugged off his jacket and removed his boots before turning the corner.

His mother leaned against the counter, sipping a cup of coffee. Her dark hair was pulled back into a tight ponytail and her eyes sparked behind the lenses of her glasses.

Weston sat at the kitchen table. Luke marveled for a moment that the wooden chair didn't splinter into toothpicks under his friend's weight. It'd been nearly a decade since Weston played professional football, but he still retained his tank-like physique. The sunlight from the windows reflected off his ranger badge, and the plate in front of him held remnants of scrambled eggs.

"I see my mother took pity on you, Weston."

His mouth quirked up. "Breakfast is the most important meal of the day."

Luke bent to kiss his mother's cheek.

"You look like you could use this." She handed him a fresh cup of coffee and winked. "I hid some breakfast before he could eat it all. I'll get you a plate."

"There's more?" Weston scraped the last of his eggs onto his fork. "Don't mind if I do."

"You've had two servings already!"

He sent her a charming grin, complete with dimples. "There's not a woman in three counties that can cook as good as you, ma'am. Can't blame a man for gobbling up every bite."

She chuckled. "You always know how to sweet-talk a lady, Weston Donovan."

Nancy quickly doled out food for the two men. Luke bowed his head and said a quick prayer before digging in. "This is fantastic, Mom. As usual."

She beamed. "Thanks, hon. I'm going outside to plan my garden. Hank finished tilling it this morning."

The screen door slapped behind her. Luke took a long sip of his coffee. "Thanks for stopping by."

"No trouble at all. Your mom's cooking is an excellent bribe." Weston cut into the flaky biscuit smothered in white gravy. "What's going on?"

"I might need your help on a case." Luke gave him the shorthand version of recent events.

Weston listened carefully, only asking questions for clarification. When he finished, his fellow ranger sat back in the chair. "Was Franny Heath Dickerson's daughter? He owns a huge ranch out this way, right?"

"Yeah. He inherited a lot of wealth from his father and grandfather. They're one of the founding families of Cardin."

"I vaguely remember hearing about her murder, but I was living on the other side of Texas at the time. Catch me up."

"Franny was shot three years ago in her home. She lived in a cabin near the lake, and the murder took place during the early-morning hours. There were no witnesses. The murder caused a big uproar in the county. Franny's father, Heath, donated—still does actually—large sums of money to political campaigns, including the sheriff, county prosecutor, mayor. You get the picture."

Weston nodded. "Go on."

Luke set his fork down. Acid burned his stomach and he pushed his half-eaten plate away. "The gun used by the perpetrator was never recovered. It's my understanding the investigator in charge of the case, Dan Carter, didn't have a lot to go on. In the hours before her murder, Franny had roughly fifty people over to her home for a birthday celebration. Wade had been at the party and was one of the last to leave. A friend whom he gave a ride home alibied him, but a couple of days after Franny's death, Wade confessed to Megan he went back to Franny's later that night."

Weston frowned. "Not good."

"No. Megan was in her final semester of law school at

the time and living in Houston. She called and asked for my help. She wanted me to talk to Wade."

"Let me guess, you didn't."

Luke shook his head. "It was pertinent information in an active murder investigation. I turned it over to the sheriff. Next thing I knew, Wade had confessed to the murder."

Megan had interpreted his decision as a betrayal. He understood why. Luke might not have meant to, but he'd hurt her. And those type of wounds were the kind that scarred and changed everything forever.

Weston fiddled with his fork. "Talk about complicated."

Luke picked up his plate and walked to the sink. "Tell me about it."

"Do you have any reason to believe Franny's case wasn't investigated properly?"

"No." He scraped the remnants of his breakfast into the trash. "But with a high-profile case like Franny's, the heat to solve it can cause even the best lawmen to make mistakes. The investigator in charge, Dan Carter, is ambitious. Solving Franny's murder endeared him to the Dickerson family and they've endorsed him in the upcoming election for sheriff."

Luke took the plate his friend extended and ran it under the water. "I would appreciate some backup on this if you've got time. This case is personal. I won't pretend otherwise. Having another set of eyes wouldn't hurt."

Weston joined Company A last year. The two men

had become friends, and Luke respected his investigative skills and straightforwardness.

"Awww, man. I'd love to help out." Weston clapped him on the back. "I'm touched you asked."

Luke's mouth twitched. "I'm already second-guessing my decision. I should've asked Grady."

Grady West was a fellow ranger in Company A. Luke had worked closely with him last year on a difficult case.

Weston grinned. "Naw, Grady's not as fun."

Luke's phone vibrated in his pocket. He wiped his hands on a dishtowel before pulling it out.

"Speaking of Grady..." Luke answered the call. "Morning. I've got you on speaker. Weston's here too."

"You missed a fantastic breakfast." Weston leaned a little closer to the phone. "Scrambled eggs, biscuits with gravy, sausage. Luke's mom cooked the full works."

Grady's groan came through the speaker. "All I had was cereal this morning."

"How come? I thought you were the cook in the family."

"I am, but I've taken a hiatus." He paused. "Tara's pregnant. We're expecting a boy in August."

Luke grinned and hollered congrats over Weston's whoop. Grady and Tara had been through a trying ordeal, and both had nearly died trying to protect Maddy, the little girl Tara had adopted. No one deserved happiness more than them.

"Thanks, guys," Grady said. "Unfortunately, morning sickness and country breakfasts don't match.

She can't stand the scent of food, so I see a lot of cereal in my future."

"No doubt." As happy as Luke was for his friend, he needed to turn back to business. "Do you have an update from forensics about June's vehicle, Grady?"

His fellow ranger sighed. "You're not going to like this."

FIVE

Forty-five minutes of searching June's bedroom and Megan was still empty-handed. She shoved a dresser drawer closed with a frustrated sigh. Her cell phone rang, the name Grace Sterling flashing on the screen. She didn't bother answering with a hello. Her best friend and the other half of Hunt & Sterling law firm had been texting all morning.

"It's not here, Grace."

Megan shifted the phone against her ear. Her gaze skipped around the bedroom, verifying she'd checked every nook and cranny. The closet, under the bed, the nightstand. None of it had gone untouched.

A slight drumming came over the line. Megan pictured Grace thrumming her manicured fingers on the antique wooden desk, a silk scarf highlighting her high cheekbones and ebony eyes, and her mouth pursed in thought.

Her friend sighed. "Are you sure it's not in her office?"

"I tore it apart last night. All I found were news articles about the case. There should be a lot more than that."

Megan crossed the room to the window. From this angle, Hank's truck was visible. Luke's stepfather was strolling the fence line near the barn. Nearing seventy, he still had the long stride of a man far more youthful. She'd already offered him coffee this morning, which he'd kindly refused.

"Have you drawn up the attorney/client agreement?" Megan asked.

"Yes. I'm going to see your brother this morning, and I'm not taking no for an answer this time."

"Good. Luke's made arrangements to question Wade later today, and I want you there. Meanwhile, I'll keep searching."

Her friend was silent for a long beat. "Megan, maybe you should back off. We can send a private investigator—"

"No. This is something I have to see through myself."

She glanced down at her hand, and a memory flashed in her mind. Her mother's blood coating her palm as the rain beat down on their rolled SUV.

Take care of Wade. Promise me, Megan.

I promise, Mama.

She squeezed her eyes shut and willed the haunting image away. If she thought of all the ways she'd failed to live up to that promise, it would cripple her. Right now, she needed to stay strong and focused.

"Do you think Luke will help?" Grace asked.

"Help is a relative term. He'll investigate June's accident, but I don't know if that will lead to the evidence." Megan crossed the room and opened June's closet. She shoved a row of clothes to the side and tapped against the wall searching for a secret compartment. "Honestly, I wouldn't involve him at all if I could avoid it. I can't be sure he won't hide things from me again."

"You know he was obligated to tell the sheriff about Wade going back to Franny's house that night."

"It goes so much deeper than that. My brother was drinking and getting into trouble. Luke knew about it, but never said anything. I didn't get the chance to set Wade on the right path before things spiraled out of control."

The betrayal burned like a hot iron as much today as it did three years ago, and Megan hit the closet wall with more force than was necessary.

Grace sighed again. "Just promise me you'll be careful."

"Of course. Talk to you soon."

She hung up, her mind already jumping to the problem at hand. She tapped all along the closet walls, but there was no hole or a secret compartment. Where was Wade's file? There should be notes, a list of interviews, and a timeline. The progress of June's investigation had to be documented somewhere.

A thump cut through the silence. Megan froze and the hair on her arms rose. It sounded as if it'd come from the living room. She scooped up her cell phone from the closet shelf, but hesitated. The front door was locked, and Hank was outside. The likelihood of someone being in the house was miniscule.

In the doorway, she listened. Not a whisper of sound. Her heart pounded as she approached the living room. Sliding along the hallway wall, she peeked around the corner. Books, previously stacked on the coffee table, littered the floor. A streak of gray whipped past her. Megan stifled a scream.

She placed a hand on her racing heart. "Archimedes, you scared me."

The cat disappeared into the spare bedroom. Rotten thing.

Megan loosened the grip on her cell phone and let out a long breath of relief. Recent events coupled with Luke's warning were making her jumpy. The lack of sleep and gallons of caffeine in her system weren't helping.

She went into the kitchen and popped a bagel in the toaster. Leaning against the counter, her gaze drifted over the room. Could June have a secret compartment somewhere else in the house? There was an attic they used for storing the Christmas decorations, but it would be difficult...

Her spine stiffened. She hadn't checked the basement. Actually, it was a bunker, built by the first owner of the house. June hated the space and had often talked of sealing it off. Still, it would make the perfect hiding spot.

Megan's sneakers slid over the tile as she rounded the

corner of the utility room. She opened the basement door. It was pitch-black inside and snapping on the light did little to change things. A shiver of apprehension raced down her spine. Megan silently chided herself. The worst thing down there was a spider.

Wind brushed against the nape of her neck. She whirled, as a large figure loomed. Two hands landed on her back and shoved.

Pain erupted along her shoulder and hip as she tumbled down the stairs. Objects whipped by in a blur. Landing in a heap at the bottom, her head rapped against the cement floor. Stars exploded across her vision.

From a distance, the door above her slammed shut. Megan moaned. She put a shaking hand to her head. Blood, warm and slick, coated her palm.

Move.

Urgency cut through her shock. She rose onto her knees, using the wall for support. The bumpy cement bit into her hand. A black object lay a short distance away.

Her phone.

On hands and knees, Megan crawled forward. The pain in her hip made her whimper. She hoped it was just bruised and not broken. The phone swam before her eyes, and she shook her head to clear her vision. She unlocked it and the screen glowed. Megan called 911, but nothing happened. The reception bars were nonexistent.

Above her, there were scraping sounds. What was he doing? Did he assume the fall alone would kill her, or would he come down to finish the job? She needed to move to a more strategic position.

Megan struggled to her feet. The bulb above her provided enough illumination so there weren't shadows in the corners. She turned, looking for a place to hide, and gasped. The entire far wall was covered in paper. Megan took a shaky step forward and instantly recognized the face in the crime-scene photograph. Franny Dickerson. From the extent of her aunt's notes, June's investigation was far bigger, far more complex than Megan could've imagined.

A giant whoosh came from above. Megan's attention shot to the door. Her heart stuttered and the hand holding the phone trembled.

Was that...was that an explosion?

Black smoke seeped into the basement through the cracks in the door like an ominous fog answering her silent question. Panic welled in her chest. Megan hobbled up the stairs. She slipped and rammed her knee on a step. Clutching the banister for support, she kept moving.

The smoke attacked her. It burned her lungs. Coughing, she lifted her shirt, stretching it over her nose and mouth. She blindly reached for the door and felt the heat of the fire through the wood. The handle burned her fingers when she twisted it. Nothing happened.

She backed up a few steps. Desperate, Megan rammed herself against the door. The wood vibrated under her shoulder but didn't give.

Tears welled in her eyes, blinding her as much as the smoke. The need for oxygen forced her back. She stumbled to the bottom of the stairs, dropped to her knees on the cement floor and sucked in a few breaths. She searched the room for something to pry open the door, even as a bigger part of her knew it was hopeless. The earlier scraping sounds suddenly made sense. Something had been pushed in front of the basement door.

A sob rose in her chest as hysteria threatened to take hold. Megan knew she should pray, but God seemed so far away. With everything she'd been through—from her parents' death to the attack on June—she was certain He didn't listen to her anymore.

The Lord helps those that help themselves.

Her aunt's saying filtered through her mind as if June was right there, whispering it in her ear. Megan shoved her terror away and willed herself to focus. Finding a way out needed all her energy.

She unlocked her phone. It flickered on before going dark. Her fingers trembled as she tried again. The screen lit up. But for how long?

Phone calls wouldn't go through, but maybe something else would work. Pulling up the text messages, she typed one out. It was garbled, the cracked screen and damaged phone making it nearly impossible. She could only hope Luke would understand.

At the top of the stairs, she hit send. The smoke was as thick as gravy and her lungs seized. Megan sputtered and coughed, the need for fresh air sending her back down the basement stairs.

This time when she tried to unlock her phone, it didn't work.

The screen stayed black.

Luke hung up the phone with Grady, his breakfast sitting like lump of coal in his stomach. The forensic team couldn't determine June's accident was caused by foul play, but he knew it was.

"I don't understand why you think it's a murder attempt." Weston leaned against the counter. "June could've accidentally put steering fluid in her brake line causing them to fail. People have done it before."

"That's what someone wants us to believe." Luke settled his hat on his head and grabbed his keys from the peg by the door. "But June was a plane mechanic in the Air Force. I've seen her fix tractors and pull apart engines. She never would've put steering fluid in her brake line."

Weston's mouth opened, but Luke's phone beeped with an incoming message, cutting him off. He glanced down at the screen to find a garbled text from Megan. Not much made sense except for two words. Help and fire.

"Megan's in trouble."

Luke bolted for his vehicle. Weston's boots pounded against the concrete behind him. They jumped in the Suburban, and he shoved his key in the ignition.

"Call in to dispatch." Luke peeled out onto the street,

his pulse beating a rapid tempo. "Tell them there's a fire at 124 Hickory Lane."

"How far out are we?"

"Three minutes."

Luke flipped on lights and siren while pushing the accelerator to the floor. Three minutes. It might as well be an eternity.

Hold on, Megs.

Horrific scenarios flickered like a movie in his head. He'd seen what fire did to a person, how it killed. Once, during his days as a trooper, he'd been called out to assist with a three-car pileup. One of the vehicles caught fire and went up in a flash before he or anyone else could render aid. The screams of the man inside still haunted his nightmares.

No. He willed the image out of his mind. That wouldn't happen. Not to Megan. Luke gripped the steering wheel until his knuckles went white. He swerved around a tractor creeping along the narrow two-lane country road.

"Tell them to send an ambulance," Luke ordered. "Hank was watching the house."

There was no way Megan was in danger and his step-father had stood by and let it happen. Weston relayed the information in clipped and even tones, but his leg bounced up and down, betraying his nerves. Luke took a curve too fast and the back end of his vehicle fishtailed before catching hold of the asphalt. Rocks pinged off the undercarriage.

Lord, please, I need to get there in time. Don't let it be too late.

He rounded the final curve and his breath caught. June's house was ablaze. Smoke belched from shattered windows and gathered in an ominous cloud around the roof. Hank's truck sat in the driveway.

"There!" Weston pointed to something in the distance, near the backside of the barn as Luke blew past it. A blot of brown in a sea of green grass. Weston yanked on the radio and confirmed to dispatch they had injured.

Luke squealed to a stop and shoved the car into park. "You take care of Hank. I'll get Megan."

Weston took off across the field. Luke raced to the back of his vehicle and opened a storage trunk. He grabbed a bottle of water and two bandanas. Soaking the fabric, he shoved one in his pocket and wrapped the other over his nose and mouth before snatching his tactical baton.

Flames flickered in the living room. Luke didn't bother trying the front door. Instead, he went around the side. The smoke leaking from the bedroom windows was wispy and thin. He smashed his baton against the windowpane and it shattered, glass spilling over the ledge to the carpet below. A dresser drawer hung askew and the closet door was wide open.

"Megs," he screamed. "Where are you?"

Calling out was dangerous. There was no way to know if the perpetrator was still in the house and it could make him a target, but Luke didn't have a choice. Saving his own neck didn't matter if Megan died.

June's cat darted out from under the bed. Luke scooped him up and gently tossed him out the window, before crossing the room. Heart pounding, he moved into the hall, keeping his gun out but pointed near the floor. The heat stole his breath. Light from the flames in the living room flickered and danced with a magnetic pull.

"Megs!"

The smoke hung like a fog. Luke pressed forward, checking each room he passed. The bathroom. The spare bedroom. Each step brought him closer to the heat and the flames. The embedded survival instinct urged him to run away. It was only sheer strength of will that kept his feet moving forward. Sweat coated the back of his shirt.

"Megs, where are you?"

A faint pounding, barely distinguishable from the crackle of the fire, caught his attention. He froze. It sounded like it was coming from the kitchen area, but there was no sign of her. The flames reached a set of living room curtains and they went up in a whoosh of heat. Luke put his arm up to block his face from the sparks and ran past.

The pounding came again. He followed the sound, darting into the utility room and dipping low to get as much of the lingering oxygen as possible. His head whacked against the washing machine.

"Luke!" The pounding came again. "In here!"

He looked up. The washing machine was blocking the doorway leading to the basement. Luke tucked his weapon into its holster. He shoved his weight against the ancient appliance and it scraped against the tile. Sweat dribbled into his eyes making them sting. The heat from the fire was crushing and coupled with the smoke made it almost impossible to breathe.

When the washing machine was shoved far enough away, he flung the door to the basement open and Megan tumbled into his arms. She was whole. Alive. Luke had every intention of keeping her that way.

Pulling the still-wet bandana from his pocket, he placed it over her nose and mouth. "Can you walk?"

She nodded. He set her upright and gripped her hand. The heat intensified the moment they stepped out of the utility room. Flames licked along three of the four living room walls, and the entire kitchen was ablaze.

Megan's eyes widened. "The fire will destroy everything."

She yanked her hand out of his and disappeared back into the utility room. He chased after her, his boots pounding on the wooden steps down into the basement.

"Megs, we need to get out of here. Now."

"Help me!" She scooped up documents from the narrow table. "It's all of June's work."

His gaze swept over the piles of papers, the photographs and maps on the wall in quick snaps. Franny Dickerson's face jumped out and the cause of her panic became obvious.

"There's no time." He grabbed her arm. "Megs, now."

He pulled her up the stairs. Heat seared his skin. The fire was spreading fast, eating its way through the house. Luke kept his hand on Megan's arm as they raced through the kitchen.

The house creaked. The bookcase in the living room tilted, falling toward them. Luke whipped around and pressed Megan against the wall, using his body to cover hers. The papers fell from her hand, scattering along the floor to be eaten by the flames.

SIX

Hours later, Luke paused outside the interview room. His throat ached, and the faint scent of smoke lingered, even after showering and changing his clothes. Down the hall, Megan limped toward the electronics rooms to observe Wade's questioning. Her soft blonde hair was swept to the side, expertly covering the gash on her forehead, and the new jeans and blouse hid the other bumps and bruises. But Luke knew they were there.

His hand tightened on the doorknob, as a rush of anger so sharp he could taste it swamped him. Megan had nearly been killed. June was lying in the hospital. His stepfather was at home resting with a mild concussion. Whoever was behind this wouldn't get away. Luke would make sure of it.

Weston joined him at the door. He squinted. "You okay? I can take this on my own."

"No." Luke sucked in a deep breath and tucked his emotions away in a steel cage. They wouldn't help him.

Right now, he had to think like a lawman. "I'm ready. The camera's rolling?"

They couldn't be on while Wade was speaking with his lawyer, but Luke wanted the questioning recorded.

"Yep," Weston said. "We're ready."

He opened the door. Wade glanced up from the table where he was seated, and their eyes locked. He'd been twenty-one when he went to prison. Three years and a conviction for murder had shorn away the soft edges of youth, leaving a hardened man with the guarded look of a hunted animal. A cut split his cheek, and a bruise bloomed next to his left eye.

Luke's resolve to remain emotionless cracked. He'd dated Megan for several years before their engagement and had grown fond of her brother during that time. Seeing Wade in prison garb, dark circles under his eyes, and his nails bitten down to the quick yanked on Luke's heart.

He forced his feet forward and took the seat across from Wade. Weston ran through the motions of the Miranda warning and the procedures necessary to start questioning.

"I've informed my client about the recent attacks on his family." Grace, Megan's law partner and Wade's lawyer, folded her manicured hands over the pad of paper in front of her. "It won't come as any surprise that much of what Megan has told you is true. These attacks are connected to Franny Dickerson's murder."

Wade's gaze never left Luke. Buried in the dark depths was stark terror. "You need to protect them."

"To do that, I need the truth. Did you kill Franny?"

The air thickened, the moment drawn out and countable in heartbeats. Luke had never dreaded nor wanted an answer more.

Wade shook his head. "No, it wasn't me."

Luke scanned the other man's face, but there was no trace of deception. The knot in his stomach twisted like a knife.

"Who did?" Weston asked.

"I don't know." Wade blew out a breath. "I wish I did."

Luke pulled out a notepad and a pen from his sport coat pocket. "Let's start at the beginning. What time did you arrive at Franny's house for the party?"

"Around nine. It was her birthday and everyone had a great time. Things broke up around midnight, and I was one of the last to leave along with Kyle."

Kyle Buchanan was the sheriff's nephew and Wade's best friend. This was all information Luke already knew, but he scribbled it down anyway. "You were giving Kyle a ride home, right?"

"Yeah. On the way to his house, Franny called Kyle to say she'd found my cell phone in the couch cushions. It must've fallen out of my pocket during the party. I hadn't even realized it was missing. When I went back to Franny's to get it..." He swallowed hard. "I found her lying on the living room floor. She'd been shot."

"What did you do?"

"I freaked out. My cell was sitting on the entryway table. I grabbed it, got in my car, and started driving. At some point, my brain kicked into gear, and I realized how much trouble I was in. I also knew no one would believe me. Not even you."

Luke stilled. "Why not?"

Wade licked his lips. "Because of my actions in the past. The bar fights. Word had gotten around about my explosive temper, and it was worse when I drank."

"Were you drinking at the party?" Weston asked.

Grace leaned forward. "The statute of limitations for a DWI have expired."

"Understood."

"Yeah, I'd been drinking. I was probably over the legal limit and shouldn't have been driving." Wade laughed, although it held no real mirth. "Ironically, Franny had been trying to get me to stop. She'd been seeing Pastor John for counseling, and she encouraged me to go."

"Why was Franny seeing Pastor John?"

"I don't know. Franny didn't often share her problems with others. Coming from a high-profile family made her cautious."

Luke made a note to contact the pastor. He hadn't known Franny was receiving counseling.

"If you didn't kill Franny, why did you confess?" Luke asked.

"Because the next morning, the phone calls started. Threatening ones. I couldn't tell who it was because they used a voice distorter, but the instructions were clear. I needed to confess to Franny's murder or Megan and June would be hurt."

Wade fingered the bruise along his eye and winced. "I didn't know how seriously to take them at first, but it was enough to give me pause about how much to say. Every day, I racked my brains, trying to figure out how to get out of the situation. June and Megan were calling every day. They both knew something was wrong. I almost told Megan the truth the last time we spoke, but chickened out halfway through. The next morning, I found my dog shot on the front porch. That terrified me. I started to wonder if my stalker was listening in on my calls."

It was possible. Spyware could've been installed on the cell phone or surveillance equipment hidden in Wade's house.

"Did you tell anyone about the dog?" Luke asked.

"I buried him on the property and told June he died suddenly. During the same conversation, she mentioned stuff had been moved in her house. She passed it off as forgetfulness, but I knew better."

Did the killer have a key to June's house? Is that how he'd gotten inside without Megan knowing? Finding out things had been moved around inside the home previously made it a greater possibility.

"You figured the stalker had been inside," Weston said, echoing Luke's thoughts.

"Yeah. When the sheriff showed up at the house later that day to question me, I confessed to a murder I didn't commit. It seemed the only way possible to protect my family from getting hurt."

Luke tapped his pen against his pad. "You told the

sheriff you were secretly in love with Franny and you were angry she didn't love you back."

He blew out a breath. "I had to come up with some reason for killing her, and it was the only one that made any sense. But I lied. We had friend-zoned each other early on. There was never anything romantic between us."

"June told Megan she'd uncovered evidence proving your innocence. Any idea what that could be?"

"It's possible she found Franny's journals. As far as I know, they disappeared on the day of her death." Wade pulled on his shirt. "Listen, I told Megan and June to stay out of it for a reason. Whoever is behind this will do anything to keep it a secret."

"Like that?" Luke pointed at the slice on Wade's cheek. "What happened?"

Wade's gaze jumped to Grace, and she nodded. "Tell them. Your sister will find out anyway."

He sighed. "I was jumped at breakfast. Some guy tried to stab me with a homemade knife."

"Someone didn't want you talking to us."

Wade nodded. "It's never happened before so my guess would be yes."

How many people had that kind of influence in a prison? Luke wanted to say the list was short, but it could be simply about finding the right prison guard or inmate for the correct price.

All of the attacks had been well planned out. The killer had prepared far in advance for contingencies but bided his time to avoid drawing attention. Whatever June had stumbled upon set things in motion. The cleanup had begun, and Luke was five steps behind.

"I'm moving you into protective custody until we have a handle on what's going on," he said.

"Forget about the evidence, Luke. I don't care about me. I just want you to protect Megan and June."

"Well, I do care about the evidence and you. Unfortunately, I can't offer any guarantees in that regards." Luke leaned forward and locked eyes with Wade. "But here's one you can take to the bank. No one will touch your family. I can promise you that."

The interview room was cold, and Megan hugged her arms around her waist. She stared at her brother. She wanted to simultaneously hug Wade and shake him until his teeth rattled.

"What were you thinking?" she asked. "Didn't you think the truth would come out at some point?"

"No. The blackmailer promised not to touch you or June as long as I confessed." Wade scrubbed his hands over his face. "Why couldn't the two of you leave things alone?"

"Because we love you."

Her throat clogged. Eight years separated them, and he'd only been six when their parents died. June's job had long hours and an erratic schedule. Megan had been the one to get Wade up for school, cook him dinner, take him to baseball practice. She'd raised him, and it had nearly killed her when he went to prison.

Wade sagged in the chair, his elbows resting on his knees and his head in his hands. "How bad is June?"

"She's strong and a fighter." She crouched down, placing a hand on his arm. "She'll pull through."

"You need to let Luke handle this, Megs. I don't want you involved."

"Too bad. This is bigger than you now, Wade. The killer went after June. Hank was injured today. You don't get to dictate the terms anymore."

She wasn't sure why she'd allowed him to in the first place. June either for that matter. Megan didn't consider herself weak, but she'd permitted her family to determine her involvement. That stopped right this minute.

A knock on the door preceded a trooper opening it. "Time's up. We've got to go."

Her brother stood. Megan rose on her tiptoes and hugged him. Tears pricked her eyes. "Stay safe, little brother."

"You too." He squeezed her tight. "Don't do anything stupid."

They separated. Megan winced as the cuffs clinked closed over her brother's wrists. In the hall, Grace wrapped an arm around her waist and they watched, together, as Wade was escorted from the building.

"Thank you for getting him to sign the attorney/client agreement this morning." Megan swiped at the dampness on her cheeks. "Wade's made some bad choices. He shouldn't have fled Franny's house without calling the police, but he doesn't deserve to spend the rest of his life in prison."

"No, but you shouldn't investigate this by yourself. It would be better if you and Luke teamed up."

As much as Megan didn't want to admit it, Grace and Wade had a point. A killer had targeted her family. She didn't want to be foolish about the risks.

"Where is Luke?"

"In the office over there with Weston." Grace gestured down the hall, her bracelets rattling. "Stay safe, hon, and call me if you need anything."

The two women hugged, and Grace left. Megan took a deep breath, pausing outside the office to square her shoulders and lift her chin. She rounded the corner, limping slightly from the pain in her knee. Luke and Weston stopped midconversation when she entered the room.

"What do you think?" she asked.

"Uhhh, I'll give you two a few minutes," Weston said, darting for the exit, surprisingly agile for a person the size of a mountain. The door clicked behind him.

Megan raised her brows. "Well?"

"He's provided no corroborating evidence, Wade's known to lie in the past, and his story has holes big enough I could drive a tractor through." Luke's gaze snagged hers. "But I believe him."

She let out the breath she was holding in a whoosh. "I want to work the investigation together."

"You aren't a law enforcement officer."

"I'm a member of Wade's defense team and that gives

me access to anything you uncover." She crossed her arms over her chest. "I also refuse to be left in the dark this time."

Last night had given her a lot of time to think, and Megan realized she'd been running. Away from Wade's conviction. From Luke's decision to hide her brother's drinking. From her own pain. It was time to stop and face things head-on.

"You hid things from me, Luke, and I don't want that to happen again. I deserved to know Wade was getting into trouble."

"And what would you have done?" He arched his brows, his tone maddeningly calm. "Quit law school? Run back home to take care of him? Wade was an adult who made his own choices. You aren't responsible for his actions."

"So what? You just don't tell me at all." The words tumbled out of her mouth, the pent-up hurt bursting out like a bull from its chute. "You stole the decision from me. You were supposed to be my best friend. How could you not tell me?"

"I was protecting you from something you couldn't change."

"But you don't know that."

She turned away and went to the window on the far side of the office. Sucked in a breath. Then another. Her hands trembled. Raindrops collected on the glass, running down the pane like tears.

"You robbed me of the chance to put things right

before Franny's murder. Maybe I could have saved Wade —saved us all—from this."

"Or maybe you would've thrown yourself in front a train that was barreling down the tracks no matter what you did." Luke came up next to her. "I've been through this with my own dad. He didn't want the help either. My mother tried for years to get him straightened out and all she got for her trouble was a mountain of debt from putting him through rehab and a petition for divorce."

"Wade isn't your dad."

His father, Patrick, had been addicted to alcohol and drugs for years. In and out of Luke's life for most of his childhood.

"Maybe not, but Wade was heading down a path I'd seen before. I'd *lived* before. Law school was your dream. It was the first thing you reached out for and took hold of all on your own. Maybe I should've told you. I just...I didn't want Wade taking you down with him."

Her heart cracked at the pain in Luke's voice. It'd be disingenuous to say his intentions didn't matter. They did. She'd avoided this conversation because it was easier to believe there was nothing but anger and hurt between them. The fire had destroyed that notion as surely as it had the evidence. In two days, he'd saved her aunt's life and now her own.

"I'm sorry," he said softly. "I never meant to hurt you."

She closed her eyes. The air shifted as Luke turned to go, but she reached out and placed a hand on his arm, holding him in place.

"I'm sorry too. I should've given you a chance to explain things before I left. I was angry and upset, but you deserved better."

His apology didn't erase the hurt, but she'd underestimated how much it would soothe the raw edges of her wounds. She hoped hers would do the same for him.

"I want to start with a fresh slate," she continued. "We work the case together and we share whatever we find without holding back. All I want is the truth."

"Me too."

His expression was strong and determined. It wouldn't be easy to let the past go, and give Luke her trust again, but she had to. Anger wasn't getting her anywhere.

"Then we have a deal." She dropped her hand. "And I suggest we start by talking to Sheriff Franklin. I want to see the case file for Franny Dickerson's murder investigation."

SEVEN

The Medina County Sheriff's Department was a squat building attached to the courthouse, nestled in the center of town. Luke held the door open for her, and Megan swiped her palms against her jeans before crossing the threshold. A caution sign sat on the tiled entryway. Lemon floor cleaner mixed with the aroma of fresh coffee and the faint scent of old socks.

The receptionist desk was empty. Voices filtered out of Sheriff Franklin's office. Megan paused. Was someone yelling?

Cindy, the sheriff's niece and his secretary, came out of the break room. Her eyes widened. "Ah, Luke—"

Sheriff Franklin's office door flew open, and Chad Dickerson stormed out. Franny's younger brother, previously slender and hardened from bull-riding, had grown bulky in the intervening years. The oversized belt buckle holding up his Wrangler's fought with his gut. The scent of sour whiskey preceded him across the room, and a several-day-old beard covered the bottom half of his face. A scar—probably caused from being on the losing end of a tussle with a bull—started at his hairline and marched down the left side of his face.

Chad spotted her and his eyes narrowed into slits. Megan's heart skipped a beat.

"You," he bellowed, charging toward her. "It's your fault I've been dragged down here."

"Don't," Luke warned, stepping into his path, his tone low and authoritative. "Not one more step."

"Screw you, Tatum. First her brother kills my sister, and now she's accusing me of somethin' I didn't do."

Luke angled his body, protecting her. The stance brought back memories of the first time she'd met him, defending a woman against her abusive husband. The fight had earned him the scar along his lip and a place in her heart.

"Megan didn't accuse you of anything."

"I'm not gonna let you run my name through the mud, after everything else," Chad continued, as if Luke hadn't spoken. "No one in this town wants you here. If you and June were attacked, maybe it was a message."

"Chad," Sheriff Franklin's voice boomed across the room. "I'll handle this."

"You'd better." Chad fixed his gaze on Luke. "Tatum, it ain't good for your job to be hanging around with the family of a murderer. Disloyalty doesn't sit well."

Luke parted his jacket so the ranger badge flashed. "Are you threatening me?"

"No one is threatening anyone." The chief deputy, Dan Carter, pushed past the sheriff and grabbed Chad by the arm. "Come on. Let's talk in the parking lot."

Chad pulled away. He ambled toward the door, stopping long enough to cast a glance in Megan's direction. The hostility glittering in his dark eyes made her blood run cold.

"See you around, *Megs*."

The door slammed behind him like a gunshot. Luke placed a hand on her arm, the warmth of his touch a sharp contrast to the chill racing through her body.

"Okay, show's over, people," Sheriff Franklin barked out. "Get back to work."

The deputies jumped into action. The sheriff gestured for Luke and Megan to follow him before turning on his heel and heading into his office. It was large enough for a conference table and bookcases. Mounted deer heads lined one wall.

Sheriff Franklin rounded his desk and stood behind it. Pushing sixty-five, he resembled an aging bulldog—barrel chested with thick jowls and slight underbite.

"What's going on with Chad?" Luke asked, after he shut the door behind them.

"The bartender from Harry's called, claiming Chad was making threats against June and Megan. I pulled him in for questioning."

"And?"

Sheriff Franklin shrugged. "Chad says he was at home during the attack on Megan and in the hours before

June's accident. I'll go to the ranch and confirm it with his father."

The sheriff gestured to the visitor chairs before taking a seat in the cracked and worn leather one behind the desk. "Listen, Luke, Chad is a hothead whose mouth works faster than his brain, but I don't believe he has the wherewithal to plan a murder."

Megan agreed. Chad had said stuff in the past and done nothing. From the way Luke's posture stayed ramrod straight, however, he didn't believe the threats were all bluster.

Someone knocked on the office door and the sheriff barked permission for them to enter.

Dan strolled in. The chief deputy had started out as a cop in Dallas before coming back five years ago to his home roots in Cardin. His dyed black hair was plastered in place with shiny gel, the color a sharp contrast to his sallow skin, and an e-cigarette poked out of the front pocket of his uniform. His gaze raked over Megan, and she resisted the urge to pull her jacket closed.

"Glad to see you weren't seriously hurt this morning, Ms. Hunt." Dan tucked his hands in his pockets and jingled some change. "I read the reports from Lieutenant Granger who took your statement. Quite a close call."

"I was lucky Luke was there."

"Two women in one week." Dan grinned. "Must be a record, Tatum."

"Not one I'm happy to have." Luke glanced at Megan. "I'd rather there be no attacks at all."

"None of us are happy about what's going on," Sheriff Franklin said. "I want to get to the bottom of it."

"I'm glad to hear you say that. Given Wade's claim of innocence combined with June's voice mail, her car accident, the attack on Megan, and the arson, I think we need to consider the possibility that all of these incidents are connected."

"Well, that's a jump if I ever heard one." Dan leaned against the desk. "June's car accident hasn't been ruled as an attempted murder, and I doubt it will be considering there was no sign of foul play. Granted, the timing of her voice mail is suspicious, and I can see why it could cause questions, but there is zero evidence thus far that the two are connected."

"What about the attack on me today?" Megan lifted her chin. "And the fact that my aunt's house was burned to the ground."

"First of all, we can't be sure the arsonist even knew you were in the house. Your vehicle was parked in the garage. It's possible you surprised him, and he pushed you down the stairs out of fear." Dan adjusted the nameplate on his uniform. "June is a private investigator. Digging into people's business is what she does for a living. These attacks could be tied to one of her other cases."

Unbelievable. He was twisting the facts to suit his own agenda. "My brother is innocent of Franny's murder."

"Megan, I can appreciate the pain your family has been through, but your brother confessed." Dan's tone was patient and he spoke slowly, as if she was hard of hearing or emotionally overwrought. "It's not unusual, after a few years in prison, for someone to change their tune and claim they're innocent."

Heat pulsed through her veins. Her gaze shot to the sheriff, but he remained silent.

"Be that as it may," Luke said. "I want to see Franny Dickerson's case file."

The tips of Dan's ears turned pink. "Are you questioning my integrity?"

Yes. Megan screamed the answer in her head but kept her lips sealed. Arguing would get them nowhere.

"I want the truth." Luke's tone was professional, but he addressed his words to the sheriff instead of Dan. "And I want to catch the person responsible for nearly killing June and Megan. Not to mention attacking my stepfather."

"And I don't?" Dan snapped. The red spots spread across his earlobes and into his cheeks. "That's insulting."

Sheriff Franklin stood. "Dan, why don't you give us a minute?"

His gaze swung to his boss. "You're dismissing me? Are you serious?"

"Yes." The sheriff drew himself up to his full height. "I am."

Dan's expression turned dark, and for a moment, Megan thought he would refuse. Sheriff Franklin leaned over and whispered something in his ear. Whatever it was, the chief deputy deflated like a balloon. Wordlessly, he left.

Before he closed the door behind him, Megan's gaze snagged his. Pure hatred flashed in Dan's eyes.

A pinprick of fear touched the back of her neck.

———

The tension in the sheriff's office dropped by five grades when Dan left the room. Luke took a deep breath and forced his posture to relax. He'd never liked the chief deputy. Something about the man made his hackles go up.

Sheriff Franklin sighed as he retook his seat.

"Please excuse my chief deputy. Dan is a good cop, and he's taking the challenge to his work personally. Before all of this, there was no reason to question our findings on the case. Wade's confession fit with the facts and was rock solid." He paused. "Megan, I want you to know, I wouldn't have arrested your brother if I hadn't had probable cause."

"Thank you, sir. That means a lot."

"I'm also going to be honest with you. I still haven't seen anything that points to a wrongful conviction, but the coincidences of these attacks makes revisiting Franny's murder a reasonable course of action. Luke, I'm happy to have your assistance on this."

He gave a sharp nod. Luke didn't technically need the sheriff's permission, but having his cooperation made things a lot easier.

Sheriff Franklin adjusted his weight in the chair and it groaned in protest. "I'm retiring at the end of this year.

Dan wants to take over my position, and in order to do so, he'll need the Dickersons' support to win the election. Reopening Franny's case will get some pushback, and I want all of it on me."

It didn't surprise Luke that the sheriff was protecting his own. Robert's integrity was a large part of the reason he'd never questioned the events around Wade's conviction until now.

The door opened, and Brent stuck his head in. "You wanted to see me, sir?"

"Come in." Sheriff Franklin waved him toward an empty chair. "Lieutenant Granger is the lead investigator on the recent fires."

Luke relaxed as his friend took a seat. Brent had taken their statements earlier this morning after the escape from June's house.

The sheriff turned to Luke. "Lieutenant Granger also assisted Chief Deputy Carter on the Franny Dickerson murder. I'm assigning him to work with you. Any questions you have can go his way."

Luke nodded. Having his friend coordinate these cases was better than he could've hoped for.

"Did you have any other suspects in Franny's murder beside Wade?" he asked.

"One. But it won't help you much. Skeeter McIntyre died two years ago in a hunting accident." Brent frowned. "A year before her death, he and Franny had been dating seriously. Skeeter didn't take their breakup well. Friends reported he hadn't given up hope on them getting back together, but Franny wasn't interested.

Their relationship caused the rift between her and her family."

Megan sat up straighter. "What rift?"

"It wasn't a big one," Brent quickly clarified. "The family disapproved of Skeeter and felt his sole interest was in Franny's money. They pressured her to cut off the relationship, and when she refused, Heath restricted her financially. Franny moved to the lake house and started working here in the evidence room. After a few months, the relationship with Skeeter soured and she broke it off. Things with her family improved."

"Did you rule out Skeeter because of Wade's confession?"

"No, he had a rock solid alibi. Skeeter was working at his uncle's property in Fort Worth that weekend. Over a dozen ranch hands confirmed it."

Luke would double-check the alibi, just to be sure, but it seemed unlikely Skeeter was involved in Franny's death.

"Wade mentioned Franny kept journals," Megan asked. "Did you recover any from the lake house?"

"No, and the Dickersons don't have them either. I'd hoped the journals would give us some insight into anyone she was having trouble with." Brent ran a hand over his bald head. "Do you think June found them?"

"There's no way to know for sure, but there wasn't a trace of them inside the vehicle with her." Luke frowned. "Is it possible the killer took them after killing Franny?"

"I suppose it is, although there was no indication the lake house was searched. We also never recovered the murder weapon. Wade claimed he threw it in the lake. We dredged it and came up empty."

Was it possible June had found the murder weapon? Luke made a mental note to review the items recovered from her vehicle one more time.

"Who called in the murder?" he asked.

"A ninety-year-old neighbor. She was walking her dog around the lake and saw the front door hanging open. The lower level of the house was a wreck from the party. None of the neighbors heard gunshots, probably because the music was still blaring. The coroner put the time of death in the early-morning hours. Franny had alcohol in her system, but not enough to be intoxicated."

"Do you have any idea why Franny was seeing Pastor John?"

Brent shook his head. "I was surprised by that. Wade's interview was the first I've heard of it. None of her friends mentioned it."

Interesting. Why had Franny kept it a secret? And why had she told Wade? Right now, they had a lot more questions than answers. Luke needed to bring himself up to date on Franny's case and fast. "I'll need to look at everything you have on the murder."

"Of course." Sheriff Franklin tilted forward in his chair. "Most of the staff has the day off tomorrow, since it's Sunday. Why don't you come back Monday morning? I'll have Cindy pull the boxes for you. You can look through everything, decide what's important, and she'll make copies."

"You don't have the case stored electronically?" Megan asked.

Sheriff Franklin frowned, the movement causing deep lines in his jowls. "Unfortunately, we had a computer virus two years ago that took out our entire system. We lost everything, and with the county struggling financially, it wasn't feasible to hire computer experts. Thankfully, I required everything to be backed up on paper, so we have everything, but the older cases haven't been re-digitized yet."

"And thank goodness you did, Sheriff." Brent shook his head. "I can't even begin to imagine the crisis we would've had if there hadn't been physical copies of the case files."

"We'll be back in on Monday morning then," Luke said.

He rose, as did Megan.

Sheriff Franklin was slower to get up. He stretched out a hand for Megan to shake. "Whatever is going on, you will have my full support. I want the truth as much as you do."

Megan clasped his meaty hand in both of hers. "Thank you, Sheriff."

"I had a soft spot for Franny. Heath Dickerson isn't an easy man, and he pushed his kids hard. Half of Chad's troubles stem from the way he was raised and the expectations placed on him. Franny was a sweet girl with a kind heart, a lot like her momma. I was glad when she applied to work here. Her family came from money, but she was a hard worker."

Brent shook Megan's hand as well. "We'll sort this out. Promise."

Luke opened the office door and placed a hand on the small of Megan's back, guiding her out. Dan waited near the receptionist desk. He said nothing as they passed by, but Luke felt the heat of the man's glare following them all the way to the parking lot.

EIGHT

Something rumbled in her ear.

Megan jolted awake. Spiral pillars arched upward from the bed frame. It took two heartbeats to orientate herself. She was at Luke's ranch in a guest bedroom. She turned her head on the pillow and got a face full of fur. Archimedes shifted and blinked his bicolored eyes. She stroked the cat, and his purring intensified.

"Go back to sleep, buddy. Yesterday was more excitement than you've seen in a month."

Rain pattered gently against the window. She grabbed her new cell phone—purchased along with a few necessities since everything she'd brought to town was destroyed in the fire.

Almost noon. She sat straight up in bed and her head spun. She'd taken one of the pain pills the emergency room doctor had given her last night. Big mistake.

Twenty minutes and a shower later, the sound of

country music and a heavenly smell drew Megan to the kitchen. Hank relaxed in a chair at the kitchen table, the paper in his hand, and a cup of coffee at his elbow. Luke's mother pulled a loaf of homemade cornbread out of the oven, setting it on the counter, before pushing her glasses up on her nose.

"There you are." Nancy smiled and wiped her hands on the polka-dotted apron tied around her waist. "Feeling better?"

"I am." The solid night of rest had gone a long way to soothing Megan's body, but did little to ease the worries running through her mind or settle the ache in her heart. "How are you feeling, Hank?"

"Fit as a fiddle, darlin'." The paper crinkled in his hand and a flush rose in his cheeks. "Although I'd like to get my hands on the son—"

"Hank Williams McGregor, don't you dare swear." Nancy shot him a scowl. "Sunday morning and you just got back from church service. My word. You know better than that."

"Sometimes there are reasons to swear, Mom." Luke appeared in the doorway. His hair was mussed, as if he'd also just crawled out of bed, but the alertness in his gaze along with the wrinkles in his slacks caused by sitting belied the notion. "Hank deserves at least one swear word after what happened yesterday."

His mother humphed as she stirred something delicious in a huge cast-iron pot on the stove. A brown-and-white mutt ambled in behind Luke.

"Hey, Jax." Megan bent to rub the old dog's ears. He licked her hand and his tail thumped the tile floor. "Why are you limping, boy?"

"Arthritis," Luke said. "He's on medication, but the rain aggravates it."

Jax stared up at her, his brown eyes full of adoration. Megan dropped a kiss on his forehead. She'd been with Luke on adoption day, and Jax was as much a part of their courtship as lazy afternoons in the hammock or ice cream splits after training the horses.

"What are we eating?" Luke asked. "It smells amazing."

"Chili." Nancy smacked his hand as he picked at the cornbread. "Lunch won't be ready for another half an hour."

Luke stole two slices and skirted around the island, out of his mom's reach. He handed one to Megan and winked. Nancy laughed.

"You're incorrigible." She grabbed butter from the fridge, along with a knife, and pushed it in Megan's direction. "How's June doing?"

"Every day is better. They're thinking she'll be out of ICU today or tomorrow. The doctors aren't making any promises because head injuries are so touch-and-go. It's all up to June on whether—" No. She wouldn't think like that. Megan took a deep breath. "—when she wakes from the coma."

"If you don't mind, once she's in a regular room, I'd like to visit. Sit with her."

"That..." Megan swallowed past the unexpected lump in her throat. "It would ease my mind a lot to know June has you there. Thank you."

Jax let out a bark, his warm body touching her leg. Megan laughed, breaking off a piece of her cornbread, and feeding it to him. "You always knew I was a soft touch."

The familiar scene sent an ache radiating through her chest. This was supposed to have been her life. The impact of the loss had been muted in Houston, but now the full force of her choices hit her like a punch to the stomach.

Luke glanced at her, and his smile dimmed. "Since lunch isn't ready, can I show you something?"

"Sure."

She followed him through the living room. Over-stuffed leather furniture was bracketed by well-chosen end tables. Glass doors leading to a wide porch stretched the entire length of the room. Nothing had changed in the last three years, not even the rustic Texas flag or the photos on the wall. It was strangely comforting.

Luke took a turn into the home office. "Did your aunt own a Glock?"

"Yes. It was her go-to weapon."

"We recovered one from the vehicle she was in. I was hoping it was the murder weapon used to kill Franny. Guess not."

Jax hobbled in and settled with a sigh on a dog bed thick enough for a king. Megan gave his ears another rub while she studied a map of the area attached to a whiteboard. She pointed to a red marker. "Is that where June had her accident?"

"Yep. That's what I wanted to show you." Luke leaned against the desk, bracing his hands on the shiny surface. "I'm trying to figure out where she was coming from. Using information from the towers her cell pinged, June turned off her phone while in Cardin at two twenty-one and didn't turn it back on until she called you at four fifteen. That's roughly two hours we can't account for. My best guess is that she went somewhere around Woodville. What I can't figure out is why she was on that road to begin with. The quickest way to Cardin from Woodville is the highway."

Megan studied the map. "If June thought she was being followed, she would've taken the more remote route to flush them out. That could also explain why she turned her cell phone off. She didn't want to be tracked."

"Do you know her passwords? Maybe she saved something on the cloud?"

"I already checked last night and there was nothing. My aunt preferred pen and paper when something was critical, or she was worried someone might be looking for it." She rocked back on her heels. "Dan isn't happy about our investigation."

Luke tilted his head. "You think he might be involved?"

"In her voice mail, my aunt said I shouldn't trust anyone, and Wade was attacked in prison. It makes me wonder."

"Be careful about jumping to conclusions, Megs.

Dan's not my favorite person, but there's no indication he's done anything wrong in this case. It's not easy to have your work questioned, especially since he's campaigning to be the next sheriff."

"Maybe that's all it is..." She blew out a breath. "I dunno. I don't trust him."

Luke's phone vibrated, and he pulled it from the clip on his belt. One glance at the screen and his expression went flat. He hit the reject button.

"Do you need to take that?" Megan asked. "I can step out."

"No, it's fine."

She squinted at him, trying to place the tone in his voice. It shouldn't matter. It was none of her business. But there was a tension in his shoulders and a hint of pain buried in his expression. It tugged at her heartstrings. Megan's palm itched with the urge to run her fingers over the line of his jaw, and the buried desire to kiss the frown from his mouth welled up.

Not going to happen. She forced her gaze back to the map and her mind to focus on the task at hand. June. Her brother. "When can we talk to Pastor John?"

"Tonight. We can go to service together and interview him afterward."

"Perfect. Do you have photographs of the accident and the things collected from the car? I'd like to look at them."

"Yep. They're on my computer."

He sat in the leather desk chair and pulled them up on screen. Megan inhaled sharply. June's vehicle was unrecognizable. A hunk of blue metal resting on rocks halfway down the ravine.

"It's a miracle she wasn't killed instantly." Megan grabbed the mouse and clicked through the photographs. "The inside looks clean. You didn't find a zip drive tucked in the side pockets or the glove box?"

"Nothing."

The photographs of the accident scene ended and individual evidence shots began. Her aunt's blouse and pants. Five keys on a Hello Kitty key chain. The shattered cell phone.

"Hold on." Megan's heart skipped a beat, as her brain caught up to her eyes. She flipped back to the picture of the keys.

"What is it?"

"There's an extra key. That's the car, the house, the office, and the barn's tack room." She pointed to each one as she ticked them off but stopped at a light gold one with a triangle cutout on top. "But that one doesn't belong to June."

He frowned. "Are you sure?"

"Positive. She's had the same set of keys since I was sixteen years old."

Luke zoomed in closer on the photograph. "It's too big to be for a safe deposit box. Maybe a storage unit?"

"She could've made a copy of the evidence." Excitement rushed through her body and she bounced on her toes. "Or even her entire investigation. How many storage unit places are there in the area?"

He quickly did a search. "Around fifty within a two

hundred mile radius. That's a doable list. I'll shoot it over to Weston and we can start calling."

Her phone vibrated in her pocket, and the rush faded as quickly as it'd come. The hospital? She yanked out her phone, but the number flashing across the screen wasn't one she recognized.

"Hello." Silence. There was breathing on the line so someone was there. The hair on the back of Megan's neck stood up. "Hello?"

Luke leaned in closer, and she angled the phone so he could hear.

"You need to leave town," a woman whispered. "It's not safe. Please go, otherwise he will kill you."

Luke tried to focus on the church service, but the desperation in the woman's voice from the phone call kept bleeding into his thoughts. It made him want to wrap Megan in bubble wrap and keep her on the ranch where she was safe.

He glanced at her out of the corner of his eye. She was singing the closing hymn, her beautiful voice lifting to the heavens. She pulled the hymnal they were sharing closer to turn the page and nudged him. A slight tease for not singing along. Luke nudged her back and Megan's lips turned up in a small smile. His gut clenched. Under ordinary circumstances, it would've been embarrassing to acknowledge how much he still cared, but nearly losing her in the fire had humbled him.

He wished there was a way to fix what was broken between them, but it was a fool's errand. Even if—and that was a big if—they proved Wade's innocence and got him out of prison, it wouldn't matter. He'd broken her trust. Luke knew from his own experiences some wounds changed a relationship forever.

The service ended, and people started filing out of the church.

"Megan? Luke?" A woman's voice came from behind and they both turned.

Rosa Crenshaw, owner of the local coffee shop and one of June's good friends, worked her way up the aisle against the flow of traffic. Trailing behind her was a younger woman, in her mid-twenties, dark hair tucked into a long braid.

Rosa embraced Megan. "Oh, hon, it's so good to see you." She pulled back and reached out a hand to affectionately pat Luke's arm in greeting. "How's June?"

"She's getting better, but progress is slow."

"We'll keep her in our prayers." Rosa gestured to the younger woman standing behind her. "I'm not sure if you remember, but this is my niece, Gerdie. She's staying with me while she applies to business school."

"Of course I remember Gerdie." Megan grinned. "Although you were a teenager when I saw you last. It's lovely to see you again."

"Thanks. You too." Her lips spread in a tight smile and her hands knotted together. "Aunt Rosa, I'm going to sign us up for the Cleantastic."

"That's right. It's next week. I almost forgot."

77

The Cleantastic was an annual event. The town got together one evening to clean the entire church from top to bottom.

"See you outside." Gerdie's dark braid bobbed as she raced down the aisle.

Rosa sighed. "I'm sorry about that. This whole thing with Franny has her in knots. They went to grade school together before Gerdie moved away with her mom after the divorce."

Megan's shoulders dropped. "Of course. It's not easy."

"Not for any of us." Rosa reached out and squeezed Megan's arm. "Bessie's been asking about June every day since the accident. Our Bible study is on Wednesdays, and it's not the same without your aunt."

Bessie Granger was Lieutenant Brent Granger's mother. Come to think of it, Luke had seen the three women huddled together at the Wake Up Cafe from time to time.

"Bessie's at the hospital so much, what with her cancer treatments and all, and I go up and sit with her when I can," Rosa continued. "We'd love to pop in on June. You will let us know when she can have visitors, won't you?"

"Of course, I will." Megan paused. "Rosa, can you think of any reason why June would've been in Woodville?"

"Woodville, you say?" Her lips pursed and she thought for a moment. "Not off the top of my head. I'll ask Bessie when I see her, though. She's got a better memory than I do for things."

"I would appreciate it."

"Of course, dear. And come see me at the cafe when you have time."

Megan sat back down in the pew with a sigh after Rosa left. "Poor Gerdie. She couldn't get away from me fast enough. I'm bringing up painful memories by digging into this case."

"You aren't doing it to hurt them."

"I don't think that makes it any easier." She jerked her chin. "Here comes Pastor John."

The pastor greeted them with a wide smile. Mid-fifties with an upbeat disposition and a mop of unruly curls, he'd been in charge of the church for two decades. Pastor John shook both of their hands and asked about their families.

"I was very sorry to hear about June's accident and the attack on you, Megan." Pastor John sat in the pew in front of them, twisting in the seat so they could face each other. "It's my understanding these events may be connected to Franny's murder. Is that true?"

"It is," Luke said. "I know the sheriff's office didn't speak to you after the murder, so we'd like to follow up."

"I was on a two-week retreat when it happened, and by the time I came back, Wade had confessed. I didn't think the information I had was important and now..."

Beside him, Megan stiffened. Luke placed a hand on her arm to prevent her from asking questions. Sometimes, it was better to let the witness lead the conversation.

"Franny started seeing me because she was conflicted about her relationship with Skeeter. They'd fallen in love, but her father and brother disapproved of the relationship."

Pastor John confirmed the information Brent had provided yesterday. Luke kept quiet because he sensed there was more.

"Franny gave in to the pressure from her family and broke up with Skeeter." The pastor ran a hand over his hair and the curls bounced away from his forehead before flopping back. "But the separation didn't last long. Living on her own and working at the sheriff's department had given Franny a taste of independence. She and Skeeter reconnected."

Luke leaned forward. "Hold on, are you saying they were dating at the time of her death?"

He nodded. "They kept it secret from everyone—even their friends. The more their love grew, though, the more difficult it became. They wanted to get married. Franny needed guidance on how to come clean to her family."

"Do you know if she told them about her relationship with Skeeter?"

"I don't believe she did. The last time we talked, she was still debating things." He paused. "Of course, I can't be sure. Franny and her mom were very close."

Megan frowned. "Was Franny worried about telling her dad and brother because she didn't want to cause strife with her family, or was there something more?"

Pastor John's gaze dropped to his hands, and he fiddled with his wedding ring. His wife worked as an accountant for the Dickerson ranch. Cardin was a small town and word could get around.

"It's just us here, Pastor," Luke said. "We aren't interested in gossiping."

The other man let out a sigh. "No, of course you aren't. Franny alluded her brother had been physical violent in the past. In fact, the reason Skeeter stopped training to be a bull-rider with Heath was because Chad accused him of cheating. There was a physical altercation between Chad and Skeeter as a result. Admittedly, I was concerned about Franny telling her family about her relationship with Skeeter, considering the animosity."

Pastor John wasn't known for creating drama or speaking out of turn. If he was worried about Chad's reaction, then Franny must've been too. But was Chad disciplined enough to plan a murder and then frame someone else for it?

"I'm very sorry," Pastor John said. "Maybe I should've come forward with the information anyway, but I didn't think it was important. I was wrong."

"You didn't know." Megan passed a glance at Luke. "We all seemed to have missed something with this case. Did you speak to my aunt about this, by any chance?"

"No. We've never talked about it. June did come to me to discuss Wade. This was before the murder, of course. I tried to reach out to your brother, but he wasn't interested. Then Franny mentioned she'd also been encouraging him to come in. Wade called while I was on the retreat. The Lord works in mysterious ways, but I often wondered if things would've turned out differently if I'd been here."

"The what-ifs..." Megan let out a breath. "They stink."

NINE

He watched through the night vision binoculars as Luke and Megan crossed the church parking lot. Sweat beaded on his forehead. Mistakes were piling up, one after another. His fingers brushed against the cold metal of his rifle. It was tempting to shoot them now, but there could be witnesses. He didn't need another screw up.

Luke's gaze swept across the parking lot. The ranger paused as if he sensed someone watching.

You can't see me, but I can see you.

Hunting was second nature to him, and he'd parked his vehicle in the shadows across the street from the church. As expected, Luke's gaze drifted over him without stopping, and a rush of adrenaline flooded his veins. Tatum was smart and irritatingly moral, but he wasn't a superhero. He was a man like any other.

And men bled.

He'd hoped to avoid killing the ranger, but the chances of that happening were over. Luke would never stop now that he suspected Wade was innocent. No, the issue wasn't whether they would die. It was how.

He imagined their heads exploding like watermelons from the force of a bullet and a sick satisfaction washed over him. Murder wasn't something he hungered for, but the last few days had filled his mind with dark thoughts and a clawing desperation. Pushed into a corner, a man would do anything. Even kill.

Luke's truck drove out of the lot, his taillights fading into the night.

Soon. It would all be taken care of soon.

TEN

Megan rubbed the cotton ball soaked in nail polish remover over June's big toe, erasing the chipped purple polish. Someone pushed a cart down the hall of the hospital, the screechy wheel loud enough to be heard through the closed door.

"After meeting with Pastor John, it's obvious Chad Dickerson could be involved. If he found out his sister was going to marry Skeeter…" She whistled. "I could see him be angry enough to confront her. Maybe Dan knows Chad has motive. Or worse, he knows Chad killed Franny and he's helping to cover it up?"

Her aunt didn't answer. June's eyelids remained closed, her hair spread across the pillow. Various tubes creeped out from under the blankets. A monitor silently tracked June's heart, the pulse steady and strong. She'd been moved out of ICU this morning, and her condition remained stable, but she hadn't woken yet.

Megan had read it was possible for coma patients to

hear things around them even if they couldn't react. Maybe it would be better to talk about sunshine and butterflies, but her aunt had never been fond of wearing rose-colored glasses. If June were awake, they'd be discussing the case.

"Then there's the mystery caller. I have no idea who she is, but I'm worried about her. She sounded terrified." Megan rummaged inside her purse and pulled out a bright-yellow nail polish. It was June's favorite color, the same shade as a sunflower. She shook it and applied the color to her aunt's toenails. "Of course, I'm not going to leave town, but don't worry, I'm not being foolish. Luke will stick to me like glue until we solve the case."

She finished the right foot and moved on to the left. "In other news, I went to church. You'd be proud of me. I thought it would be weird since I haven't attended service since Wade's arrest, but it wasn't. It was...comforting."

That had surprised her as had the way her heart longed to go back. Something about singing the hymns and hearing the Bible readings had settled her. As if she'd been on a long journey, lost and wandering, only to unexpectedly find her way home.

"Almost done." Megan did a final swipe with the polish and took a step back to admire her work. "There. Beautiful. I don't want you to wake up and see chipped nail polish on your feet. It would drive you insane."

She slipped her hand into her aunt's and watched the rhythmic rise and fall of her chest. June was breathing on her own, a good sign, but things were still iffy. Either she would wake from the coma or she would slip into a vegetative state. A drop landed on their joined hands and Megan realized she was crying. She bit her lip.

God, I know we haven't talked in a long time, but I'm lost. I've been lost. And I could use some help here.

As far as prayers went, it wasn't great. And nothing dramatic happened, like June opening her eyes or twitching her fingers, but considering Megan hadn't talked to God in three years, it felt like a huge step forward.

She spent another twenty minutes with her aunt before kissing her cheek and going out into the hall. Luke was chatting with the trooper standing guard outside June's room. He shook the man's hand before intercepting her. "Ready?"

"Yeah. I'll come back tonight again to check on her. Thanks for waiting."

"I don't mind." He shoved his hands in his pockets. "Mom's on her way. She's bringing a book to read to June, but I was afraid to ask which one. Your aunt may wake up knowing how to make Baked Alaska or with a newfound love of romance novels."

Megan chuckled. "Considering June doesn't know how to make grilled cheese without burning it, I'd love for some of your mom's cooking skills to rub off on her."

He laughed and the sound sent a warmth spreading through her. As much as she wanted to keep the boundaries up between them, each moment in his presence made it harder.

"I saw the doctor speaking with you earlier." Luke pushed the button to call the elevator. "Any change?"

"No." She dug around in her purse. Her fingers brushed against plastic and she yanked out a bag of jelly beans. "Although I'm taking the move out of ICU as a good sign. June didn't have many injuries, which is surprising considering the car sailed into a ravine. The head trauma is the most serious, and we just have to be patient."

She opened the bag and held it out. "There are a lot of red ones."

The old joke earned her a heart-stopping smile. Luke claimed he only liked red jelly beans and, when they were dating, ate all the cherry-flavored ones out of her packages.

"Thanks." He plucked out a few. "Sheriff Franklin sent a message and asked for more time to find Franny's file. The storage room is a cavern, so I'm not surprised. Want to run by and talk to Kyle now?"

"That would be great."

Kyle was her brother's best friend and had been with Wade on the night of Franny's murder.

She popped a few more jelly beans in her mouth. "Could we stop by June's house first? I want to grab the saddles from the tack room. The lock on the door isn't great and I don't want them stolen."

Luke had collected Cinnamon on Sunday morning while Megan was still asleep and brought the horse to his ranch, but he hadn't known to collect the saddles too.

"Sure." He zipped up his jacket as they exited the hospital. "That's a good idea."

In the car, she checked her emails on her phone, but thankfully, there was nothing pressing.

"How long will you be able to stay in town?" Luke asked. "It can't be easy to juggle your cases from here."

"It's not, but Grace has taken over for me. One benefit of a partner is that we share the caseload and help each other out when personal matters get in the way. My goal is to stay as long as necessary to get June well and this case solved."

Both things could take a long time, but thinking too far ahead was draining. Megan would deal with it one day at a time.

"I'm curious, how do you decide which clients to represent?" He took the exit off the freeway toward June's house. "A lot of criminals claim to be innocent."

"True. Grace and I research each case before agreeing to represent it. We never want to help anyone guilty of murder. At the same time, the system isn't perfect and sometimes innocent people end up behind bars for crimes they didn't commit." She paused. "June does the same with her cases. She handles insurance fraud and stuff like that to pay the bills, but there were criminal cases she was passionate about."

He tapped his thumb against the steering wheel. "I wish June had talked to me about her investigation."

"My aunt is stubborn, independent, and protective. She wouldn't have done anything to put your career in jeopardy. Without proof of Wade's innocence, reopening

Franny's case would've set off a hornet's nest of issues for you."

Luke blew out a breath. "That's...irritating."

"Isn't it?" She tossed him a look. "Pot meet kettle."

He rolled his eyes and his mouth twitched. "Yeah, yeah. I got it."

Her aunt's house came into view and Megan inhaled sharply. The destruction was extensive, and the closer Luke drove, the worse it got. The chimney stuck out, a lone sentinel, protecting broken wood and blackened bricks. The plants in the front yard had been trampled. The roof, damaged by the fire and the water from the fire hoses, caved inward. Everything her aunt had worked for was gone. June would be devastated.

Luke parked in the driveway, and his hand closed over hers. Strong and warm, his touch was gentle and grounding.

"It sucks, Megs, no doubt. But she can rebuild."

She closed her eyes, shoring up her emotions. There would be time to grieve later. Right now, getting her brother out of prison and her aunt well required all her emotional energy.

Megan squeezed his hand. "I know. And it's only stuff. The most important thing is that no one was hurt."

She glanced at Luke and their eyes caught and held. It became hard to pull air into her lungs. Her emotions were all tangled together. Years of friendship and love didn't disappear, no matter how much she'd tried to make them. If he'd died saving June...or her...

"Come on." Luke jerked his hand away from hers. "Let's get the saddles."

She swallowed hard and fumbled with the door handle. The slap of cold air was a welcome relief, cooling her heated cheeks. They walked across the yard in silence.

The air inside the barn was scented with hay, leather, and horse. Megan took a deep breath. Whenever she was troubled, this was the place she went. Her hand traced over the worn wood of a stall door on the way to the tack room.

She pulled out her spare set of keys and shoved the right one in the lock, but the door to the tack room swung open on its own. Her heart skipped a beat.

She hurried to flip on the light, relieved to see the saddles untouched. Hers was on the far right, the leather polished and clean. *Oh, June.* It'd been three years since Megan had used the saddle, yet her aunt kept it prepared and ready.

"Megs, don't touch anything."

Luke's order sent chills down her spine. She turned and gasped. Written on the wall in blood-red letters was a warning.

Keep digging around and you'll die.

The perpetrator was hoping to scare Megan off, or deter the investigation, but every threat backfired. It fueled Luke's determination to get to the truth.

"The paint's dry. There's no way to know how long it's been here, Luke." Brent hitched up his duty belt and stepped back to survey the horrible message. Static came out of the portable radio on his shoulder before cutting off. "We don't even know if it was meant for Megan. It could've been a warning for June."

"Except she never reported it."

"That doesn't mean anything. I know for a fact, June received threats a couple of years ago on another case she was working, and she never reported those either."

"He's right," Megan said. She stood with her hands on her hips, eyeing the message, fury glimmering in her eyes. "June might not have told anyone. And I haven't been in this room since arriving in town."

"Spray-painting the threat seems to be the main purpose for jimmying the lock." Brent pointed to the saddles. "Those are still here, so the perpetrator wasn't after a quick buck. Fingerprinting might not yield us anything, but I'll get the kit from my car and try anyway."

He strolled out of the tack room.

"I touched the door handle. Even if there were fingerprints, I've probably smeared them." Megan yanked the clip from her hair, sending it cascading down her shoulders in a golden wave, and rubbed her scalp. "If the perpetrator thinks this will make me back down, he's got another thing coming. I'm not going anywhere."

"You mean, we," Luke said. "We're not going anywhere."

The tension in her body eased. Her lips curled into a smile that kicked his pulse up a notch. "Right."

Brent re-entered with a field kit. "Hey, dispatch told me they've located Franny's case file. I'm gonna need some time here, but you don't have to wait. Why don't you guys go on ahead?"

"We were going to take the saddles over to my ranch," Luke said.

"I'll do it after I'm done. Megan, I'll need to collect your prints to exclude them, but we can do that later."

"Thanks, Brent."

During the short drive, Luke's mind twisted with various possibilities. The warning on the tack room wall was amateurish and silly. It didn't fit with the carefully planned attacks carried out on June and Megan. Nothing about this was adding up or making sense.

He pulled into the parking lot at the sheriff's department and rounded the vehicle to open Megan's door.

"Let's go over to the pharmacy and talk to Kyle first, as we'd planned," he said. "His property butts against June's. Maybe he's noticed someone hanging around in the last couple of weeks."

As they made their way down the sidewalk, Luke noticed her gait wasn't even. "Is your leg bothering you? Let's go back. We can drive—"

"No, it's just a bit sore. I'll be fine."

Stubborn woman probably wasn't taking her pain meds. He offered his arm. Megan hesitated before sliding her hand into the crook at his elbow. Heat radiated out from the point of contact, wiping away any trace of a chill from the February air.

Luke knew he should keep a firm distance, but

recalling the look on Megan's face while they were talking in front of June's house pushed logic to the wayside. In the depths of her green eyes, he'd seen an echo of the love they'd once shared. It weakened his resolve, and he'd been tempted to lean over and kiss her.

The same feeling, along with a host of memories, tugged at him as they strolled down the sidewalk. Megan's hair shimmered like spun gold in the sunlight, and when she smiled up at him, Luke felt like a superhero. He needed to get control of this before his heart ended up in serious trouble.

The pharmacy was on the corner and the automatic doors slid open when they approached. Every head in the place turned in their direction. Luke ignored the stares and beelined for the back counter where prescriptions were filled. Kyle caught sight of them and stiffened. His narrow shoulders and mop of shaggy hair made him look more like a teenager than a man in his twenties.

"Luke. Megan. What can I do for ya?"

"Hi." Luke greeted him with a smile. "Sorry to drop in on you, but I have some questions about a couple of incidents that happened on June's property."

"I don't know anything about the fire." His voice, thickened by a Southern drawl, was loud enough to carry across the store. "I wasn't home when it happened. I was here."

"I'd still—Oof!"

Luke cut off as Megan's elbow jabbed him in the ribs. He glared at her.

"Sorry. I was trying to find something in my bag." She

smiled sweetly before setting her purse on the counter and rummaging around inside. "I have a question about something else. June's doctor at the hospital wants to change her thyroid medication. Can you explain the possible side effects?"

Luke glanced over his shoulder. Mrs. Patchinson, the elementary school principal, pretended to study a box of cold medicine while eavesdropping. An employee in the next aisle had edged closer, still holding the same magazine from earlier.

He shot them both a glare, but it had no effect.

Kyle went into a short spiel about the medicine and picked up his pen. "I'll write some of this down for you. That way it'll be easier to discuss with the doctor."

Megan nodded. "That'd be great."

He scribbled on her paper before folding it over and handing it back. "Is there anything else?"

"No, that's it. Thanks."

Megan nudged Luke, more gently this time, and headed for the door. The heat of everyone's stare seemed to bore into their backs. He followed her around the corner and out of potential eyesight range.

She opened the note. "Kyle says to meet him in the alley behind the hair salon in ten minutes."

"This is ridiculous."

She let out a half laugh and slipped her hand back into the crook of his elbow. "This is small-town politics. I would've thought you'd be better at it by now."

"I've only lived here for seven years. Maybe I need another seven to understand it." His mouth twitched.

"You've been away for three years but fall right back into it like a duck to water."

"I grew up here. That makes a difference." She shook her head. "How does June stand it? The looks and whispers. The hostility. It's already making my skin itch."

"I think it was tough for a while, but things died down. We've kicked it all off again with the investigation."

"I suppose. It's easier in Houston. No one knows who I am or who Wade is, unless I tell them."

She turned on Hill, probably to avoid Main Street and more townspeople. Huge elm trees lined the wide street and the shouts of children from the nearby park carried on the wind. They ducked into the alley behind the Clip and Curl.

A few minutes later, Kyle joined them. He'd traded his white lab coat for a leather jacket and, judging from the black boots accented with chains on his feet, was still fond of riding his motorcycle as much as the weather permitted.

"Is it true?" he asked, without preamble. "Is it possible Wade is innocent?"

"It's what we're trying to determined," Luke said. "Why? Would it surprise you if he was?"

"I...I don't know. I had a hard time believing Wade would've killed Franny. They had a good friendship. I mean, they flirted, but it never struck me as anything serious. Then he confessed, so that changed things."

"Have you noticed anyone lingering around June's property in the past couple of weeks?"

Kyle's gaze skittered away, and he shoved his hands in the pockets of his leather jacket. "Nope."

"You sure?" Luke had the faintest sensation Kyle wasn't being honest. "It might not have been recently. Could've been even as far back as a couple of months."

"Naw. There are a lot of woods separating our properties, so it'd be hard for me to keep track of the comings and goings at June's house."

Megan frowned. "Wade said he gave you a lift home from the party that night and along the way, Franny called to say she'd found his cell phone. Is that true?"

"Yeah. He arranged to go back to her place to pick it up after dropping me off." Kyle shifted his weight back and forth. "Listen, Megs, there's something you should know."

"What?"

"About ten minutes after Wade dropped me, I got a phone call from Franny. She didn't say anything, but I could hear voices. At the time, I figured she'd butt-dialed me or something, and I hung up. It wasn't until later I realized the significance of what I'd heard. Someone else was there with her that night."

"How can you be sure someone was there?" Luke asked. "Maybe it was the television."

"No, it was definitely a person and they were having a conversation. I know the difference."

It would've taken a good twenty minutes for Wade to get back to Franny's house after dropping Kyle off, even if he floored it. It couldn't have been Wade she was talking to.

"Was it a man or a woman?" he asked.

"It sounded like a man, but I can't be sure. The voices were muffled." He shifted his weight again. "I told Dan about it right after the murder, and then June came to my house asking all kinds of questions. I told her too. Other than that, no one else knows. When Wade confessed, I was surprised. I'd convinced myself I must've been mistaken about what I heard that night. But with these attacks...now everything is different. Maybe Wade is innocent after all."

ELEVEN

Kyle's revelation plagued Luke for the next day and a half. Knowing someone was with Franny near the time of her murder didn't prove Wade's innocence, but it was significant. The more Luke dug into the case, the deeper his doubts went.

Weston leaned back in his chair and it groaned. "Any idea who was with Franny on the night of her murder?"

"None," Luke said.

It was lunchtime, and the Medina County Sheriff's Department was bustling with activity. The door of the conference room was cocked open and, a riot of laughter came from a small group of deputies gathered around a pizza box on someone's desk.

Megan frowned. "Maybe we shouldn't discuss this with the door open."

"Good point." Luke got up and shut it. "I had troopers recanvass the neighbors around the lake, but no one remembers anything. We also questioned a few of

Franny's girlfriends, but they confirmed everyone left the party around the same time."

"We don't even know whether it was a man or a woman," Megan added. "So the information is helpful, because it proves someone else was there, but narrowing it down will be difficult."

Weston eyed the table covered in documents and photographs. "What is all of this?"

"It's Franny Dickerson's case file."

"Why is it such a mess?"

Megan blew a strand of hair out of her face and pushed down on a hole punch. It squeaked in protest. "When we opened the boxes, it looked like someone had dumped all the pages on the floor before shoving them back inside and closing the lid."

Weston's eyes widened, and he shared a look with Luke. Neither man said anything, but they didn't have to. They'd worked with enough departments to recognize potential trouble.

"It took us all afternoon yesterday just to put it in some kind of order," Megan continued. She placed the pages in a binder and added a divider. "Today, we're working on making copies."

"What news do you have?" Luke asked.

"Well, your mysterious caller, Megan, used a prepaid phone," Weston declared. "Not much of a surprise there. I got a warrant to ping the phone to come up with a general location, but it's been turned off. Chances are the person bought it for this purpose and only turns it on to make a call."

Luke frowned. Identifying the woman through her phone had been a long shot, but it was still frustrating to hit another brick wall.

Megan pushed down on the hole punch and it squeaked again. "So there's no way to find out who she is?"

"Not at the moment. Record the call next time. That would give us her voice to analyze."

Luke punched his own set of sheets and tucked them into a binder. "What about the key we found on June's key ring? Any luck there?"

"I'm afraid not." Weston scowled. "I even expanded the search to any storage unit within a four hundred-mile radius. None of them use a key like the one June had."

"What else could it be for?" Megan asked.

"Well, I had someone at the lab take a look. The key could be for almost anything. The lock it goes to is commonly sold at hardware stores."

The conference room door opened and Cindy bustled in. The sheriff had hired his niece as his secretary after she finished college several years ago. Her ash-blonde hair was pulled back in a neat ponytail and her floral dress was feminine and understated. Cindy was young but ran the office with graceful efficiency.

She set a neat stack of papers down on the table. "Okay, here's the final batch of interviews. The copier has been on the fritz and the repairman just arrived, so I'll take a small break while he looks at the machine."

"Thank you, Cindy." Megan lifted the hole punch. "And I hate to ask, but if you get a chance, can you rustle up another one of these? This one is on its last leg."

"Sure thing. If you need anything else, give a holler."

She closed the door gently behind her.

Megan reached across Luke to shift the new pages closer to her and he caught a whiff of her honeysuckle perfume. The soft pink sweater brought out the color in her cheeks and made her green eyes shimmer like emeralds. Her arm brushed across his knuckles. Luke's pulse jumped, and he moved back to give her more room.

"So..." Weston wagged his eyebrows. "As happy as I am to give you folks an update, this is all stuff we coulda talked about on the phone. Luke, you mentioned you needed to have something delivered to the lab?"

"Yeah." He went to the end of the table and found the right evidence bag. "These are the bullets used to kill Franny. They were never sent to the state lab for testing because Wade confessed. I'm hoping we can get good striations."

"But the gun used to shoot her was never found," Megan said.

"Yes, but that doesn't mean we won't find it. There's also a possibility Franny's killer has used the gun in another crime. If we're lucky, the striations from these bullets will be in the database."

When bullets were shot, the barrel of the gun created grooves and nicks also known as striations. They were as unique as a fingerprint. Luke hoped they could lead to a suspect.

"You called me on a good day. I was heading to the

lab with evidence on another case I'm investigating." Weston checked his watch. "I'd better get a move on."

Megan smiled sweetly. "You mean, you don't want to stay and help us with all of this?"

"I'd love to, doll, but paperwork and I are like oil and vinegar." He picked up the evidence bag before tipping his hat and flashing his dimples. "Besides, who would get your bullets to the lab?"

Doll? Luke shot his friend a glare, but Weston's smile only widened. Oh, it was on.

"Megs, did I ever tell you the story about how Weston tried to subdue a subject with pepper spray and ended up hitting another trooper instead?"

Her mouth dropped open. "Seriously?"

"Yep." Luke grinned. "He followed that doozy up a day later by getting locked out of his patrol car."

Weston glowered, but there was no real heat behind it. "In my defense, I had the flu that week."

"That's a good excuse." Megan pressed her lips together, probably smothering a chuckle. "How long did it take before the trooper you pepper-sprayed talked to you again?"

"It only took a week because he got revenge. At a training seminar, they needed a volunteer to be zapped by a Taser. He told the whole class about what I'd done. Guess who ended up being the guinea pig."

They all laughed. Weston tipped his hat to Megan one more time before they went into the bullpen to handle paperwork for the evidence transfer. Luke walked him out to the parking lot.

"Megan's nice. And smart," Weston said. "Ain't too bad on the eyes either—"

"If you don't want to be kissing the concrete, I'd stop right there."

Weston chuckled. "Don't get all riled up. I just understand why you put a ring on her finger."

Any man in his right mind would. He nearly said the words aloud before catching himself. Nope, he wasn't going down that road. Still, a sharp pang struck his chest at the thought of Megan married to someone else.

Weston pinched his lips together and scanned the parking lot. It was empty. His fellow ranger took a step closer to him. "What's with the evidence being all messed up?"

"I don't know yet. Could be a simple mistake..." Luke tucked his hands in his pockets. "Still, I'm not sure everyone in the sheriff's department is on our side. The real question is why?"

Megan paused from fighting with the hole punch and stretched her cramped muscles. The window in the conference room overlooked the parking lot, and she glimpsed Luke talking with Weston.

Both of the rangers were handsome, but her gaze lingered on her ex. She rarely had a chance to look at him when he wasn't aware. Her eyes trailed over his broad shoulders, the strength in his hands, the cut of his jaw. Luke wore authority—even while in casual conversation

—like a second skin, but there was no hint of arrogance. It was a simple confidence, as natural as breathing, and it was as attractive to her now as it had been when they first met.

She needed to be careful. Returning home had cracked open a door she'd thought was closed and bolted long ago. She couldn't allow herself to fall back in love with Luke. Too many complications and too much hurt existed between them for it to ever work.

Megan tucked the last of the reports into the binder and scanned them. The one she was looking for wasn't there. She flipped through all the sheets again, just to be sure, before stepping out of the conference room.

The door to Sheriff Franklin's office was open. He looked up from a document when she approached, peering at her over the tops of the reading glasses perched on his nose. "You looking for me?"

She pointed to the desk right outside his office. "Cindy actually."

"Try the copier room. That's where she was when I saw her last."

She turned and went down the hall. Voices filtered out of the last room along with the heavenly scent of pulled pork and barbecue sauce. Megan's stomach growled. It was well past lunchtime. She rounded the corner, surprised to find Lieutenant Granger hugging Cindy.

"Oh, I'm sorry." Her gaze skittered away as she tried to back out of the room. "I'll—"

"No, no, Megs. It's okay." Brent released Cindy and

lifted the takeout bag in his hand. "I brought my wife her favorite lunch and she can't stop herself from thanking me."

"I didn't know the two of you were married. How did I miss that?"

"You've been out of touch with things around Cardin. Not that I blame you." Color rose high in Cindy's cheeks, and she flashed her wedding band. "Tomorrow is our one-year anniversary."

"Congratulations to both of you. That's lovely. Well, now I feel worse for popping in and ruining a romantic moment."

"Don't be silly. We're at work." She shoved her husband slightly. "Not the time or the place to be canoodling with my husband."

"Anytime is a good time to canoodle with your husband." Brent laughed and hitched up his duty belt. "Were you looking for me, Megan? Or my lovely wife?"

"Cindy. I've been through all the copies you gave me, but there seems to be some interviews missing."

"Are you sure? Which one are you looking for?"

Megan didn't pause. "Skeeter McIntyre."

Her palms were sweaty, but she resisted the urge to wipe them against her pants. Not while Cindy and Brent were both looking at her. Heaven help her, she almost never lied, but it didn't seem smart to mention it was actually Chad Dickerson's interview that was missing.

"How strange." Cindy put a finger to her lips as she glanced over her shoulder at the stack of papers on the table next to the copier. "I'm certain I pulled all the interviews out when I organized everything. Brent, is it possible there's another box down in storage?"

"I suppose so. I don't remember how many we ended up with."

"Come on, Megan." Cindy grabbed a set of keys from the table. "Let's go look."

They walked down the hall, taking a turn past the break room. Cindy unlocked a door and fluorescent lights flickered on. Rows upon rows of metal shelves lined the space, filled to the brim with boxes.

"Wow," Megan said. "That's a lot for such a small county."

"It's all the cases going back to the 1900s. Plus we share storage space with the courthouse, so there are a lot of duplicates." Cindy's heels clipped against the cement floor. "For a while, we were working with the Historical Society and digitizing our old files. That's what Franny was hired to do. When she died... well, the project was abandoned. I think my uncle and the chief deputy didn't have the heart to find a replacement."

"It seems everyone really liked Franny."

"They did. She was sweet and thoughtful. Franny was a couple of years behind me in school, so I didn't know her very well until she started working here. I was suspicious at first—I figured Uncle Robert had only hired her because of her family connections—but Franny won me over. She loved history, especially when it came to the town."

The more Megan learned about Franny, the more she liked her and the more emotionally entrenched she became in the case. It wasn't enough just to free her brother. She wanted to get justice for Franny too.

"Did you attend her birthday party?" Megan asked.

"Yeah, most of the department did. We all liked her. I drove my brother there, but I left early. That's why Kyle had to get a ride with Wade home."

The workings of a small town meant people were connected in more ways than one. Kyle was Wade's best friend, but he was also the sheriff's nephew and Cindy's little brother.

"It should be right here." Cindy tilted her head back, running a manicured finger along the middle shelf. She stopped at an empty space big enough for several boxes. "Nope. I grabbed them all."

Megan glanced around the towering shelves. "Is it possible it's been misplaced?"

"I'd like to say no, but it wouldn't be the first time. Let me run upstairs and double-check the records." She hurried down the aisle. "Be back in a jiff."

Silence descended. Being alone in the cavernous space was a bit creepy. Megan wrapped her arms around her middle, and ran her palms over her shirt sleeves to ward off goosebumps. Her tennis shoes made no sound as she walked the length of the shelf, scanning the boxes for any sign of the Dickerson name. If she was going to wait, she might as well be useful.

Footsteps echoed across the space and Megan froze. They were too heavy to be Cindy's. The sound of boxes being shuffled followed. She poked her head out and glimpsed a brown uniform.

"Who's there?" A familiar voice barked out.

Megan closed her eyes. Of all the bad luck... She stepped out from behind the shelf.

The chief deputy glared at her. "What are you doing down here?"

"I'm waiting for Cindy. She's checking something on the computer."

"She shouldn't have left you by yourself," Dan snapped. He moved closer. "You shouldn't be here at all. You aren't law enforcement and you have no business accessing our records."

"I'm a part of Wade's legal team. As such, I have the right to access Franny's case file."

"Not without a court order, you don't."

A technicality. Dan knew as well as she did, the court would order the sheriff's department to turn over everything. Sheriff Franklin was just making things easier and speeding up the process. But something in Dan's expression stopped the words from coming out of her mouth.

"You think you can come in here and insult me." He scowled. "Dig through my case and cast a cloud over my good name."

Dan stepped even closer. Megan stood her ground, even as her heart rate skyrocketed. She was trapped between shelves, the exit behind him. "Back off, Dan. I want to leave."

"What about the Dickerson family, huh?" he asked, continuing as if she hadn't spoken. "Did you think about them before starting this little crusade of yours?"

The barb found its mark, and Megan cringed. She

didn't want to cause anyone pain, especially the Dickerson family.

"I know the game you're playing." He sneered. "But Luke can't change the facts. Your brother is a murderer, plain and simple. I'm not going to stand by and let you convince people otherwise."

Was that a threat? It certainly felt like one. She forced herself to meet his eyes. The hatred she found in their dark depths sent shivers down her spine.

She jutted her chin up. "I said I want to leave."

"Get away from her, Dan, before I physically remove you myself."

Megan turned her head. Luke strolled toward them, his hands balled into fists, his muscles rigid. His entire focus was on the chief deputy and the fury in his gaze was downright terrifying.

Dan jumped back, lifting his hands. "We were just having a friendly conversation."

"Stay away from her." Luke put himself between her and the other man. "We aren't out to get you, despite what you think. But if I see you near Megan again, I will make it my mission to ensure you never become sheriff in this county. Are we clear?"

Dan's cheeks heated, and he took another step back. "You don't frighten me, Tatum."

Luke's mouth flattened into a hard line. "Threaten her again, and you'll find out just how scary I can be."

TWELVE

"He threatened her?" Lieutenant Vikki Rodriguez asked, leaning forward in her chair. "The chief deputy?"

Luke nodded sharply. "Yes, ma'am. He did."

The memory of Dan's words made his stomach churn and his body temperature rise. He'd dropped Megan off at the ranch and come straight to his boss. The implications of the events in Cardin could not be ignored.

Vikki's dark lips went pale as she pressed them together. Lieutenant Rodriguez, head of the Company A ranger division working out of the Huntsville, had spent a large portion of her career as an investigator in the sex-crimes unit. She understood violence against women and the insidious forms it took better than most.

The faces of the others gathered around the conference table were equally grim. Weston sat on Luke's left, his bulky form barely able to squeeze into the chair. Grady sat on the other side of the table, his attention focused on their conversation even though his cell phone rested on the table. His pregnant wife, Tara, had a doctor's appointment today, and Grady was waiting for her call.

"What did Sheriff Franklin say when you reported it?" Weston asked.

"He showed no interest in gathering the facts regarding the incident." Luke kept his voice calm and his posture relaxed, but discussing the conversation with Sheriff Franklin sent a fresh wave of anger pulsing through his veins. "He also said Dan was under a lot of pressure and I must have misinterpreted the conversation."

"Is it possible you did?" Lieutenant Rodriguez asked.

"No, ma'am. Megan specifically told him she wanted to leave, and he was blocking her from doing so. The chief deputy was attempting to intimate and scare her."

"I trust you, Luke, and your impressions." She held his gaze. "But considering the relationship between you and Megan, it would be irresponsible if I didn't ask the question."

"Understood." He forced his shoulders to relax. "My investigation is hitting some nerves in Cardin and things are getting messy."

"Clearly. Do you think Chief Deputy Carter is involved in the Dickerson murder in some way?"

"I'm not sure. Medina County is small and people are already talking. Dan wants to be the next sheriff, and it could simply be he's sensitive about how he's perceived. However, based on my conversation with Pastor John, there could be more to it. If Chad is involved in Franny's murder, then it's possible Dan knows and is covering it up."

She brushed a strand of black hair off her forehead, tucking it back into the knot at the nape of her neck. "Do you have any evidence that's the case?"

"Not directly, but an entire box of evidence is missing. The initial interview Chad Dickerson gave after his sister's murder is also gone. It's my intention to leave this office and head straight over to the Dickerson ranch to interview Chad. That alone may create some heat, not just from Medina County but potentially from the mayor, the governor, and so on."

"Heath Dickerson has his fingers in a lot of pies."

"Yes, Lieutenant, he does."

"That doesn't make him, or his son, above the law." Her chin jutted up. "Luke, proceed with your investigation and follow the evidence. Whatever we need to do to support you, we will."

"Wow." Grace tucked her hands into the pockets of her thick wool coat. "Dan sounds like a real peach."

"Oh, he is." Megan's breath fogged in the cold air and grass crunched under her feet. Jax hobbled alongside her, and she slowed her steps so the old dog could keep up. "Did you find out anything from the background check?"

"Nothing big yet. Dan worked for Dallas Police Department for fifteen years, mostly in narcotics. Married once and divorced. No kids. Mother and father are both deceased. From what I can tell, he was on the fast track. He'd closed a couple of high-profile drug cases and was about to make captain, but then he resigned and moved to Cardin."

Megan adjusted her scarf. "Because Sheriff Franklin offered him a job?"

"Could be. Sheriffs hold office for six years in Texas and Dan moved here five years ago. I wouldn't be surprised if Sheriff Franklin wooed him here under the promise that Dan would succeed him. Still, I want to be sure, so I'm digging. Have you found anything in Franny Dickerson's case file?"

"No. Everything I have so far looks straightforward. Of course, there is an entire box missing so who knows what else has been removed. Luke's meeting with his boss and then going to interview Chad. Maybe something will come out of that, although I'm not holding my breath."

They reached the fence line and stopped. In the pasture, several horses grazed. A brilliant Texas sunset painted the sky with soft pinks and pale purples. Jax wandered farther down to sniff the grass.

"I'd forgotten how beautiful it is here." Grace rested her arms on the fence. "I always loved visiting when we had breaks from law school."

Megan pulled an apple from her coat pocket and clicked her tongue. Her aunt's horse, Cinnamon, picked her head up.

"Come on, girl. I have a treat for you."

The gorgeous brown quarter horse ambled over. Grace stroked her neck while Megan fed her the apple.

"I love the white blaze on her nose," Grace said. "She reminds me a little of your old horse, Fiona."

"Yeah, but she has the personality of her daddy Remnant." Megan wiped her hand on the leg of her jeans. "Spunky and just a touch wild."

"Well, Cinnamon certainly seems happy with her mini-vacation here. How many horses does Luke have?"

"I'm not sure. I haven't been down to the barn at all." Megan shoved her hands into her pockets to warm them. "Thanks for taking over my cases for the last week, on top of what you are doing for Wade. I don't know what I would've done if I'd had to juggle everything. If I haven't said it lately, you're amazing."

"I know." Grace linked her arm in the crook of Megan's elbow. "But it's always nice to hear."

They laughed. Megan whistled for Jax, and they headed back to the house.

Inside, Nancy was humming to herself and working on the computer. She smiled when they walked in. "You're just in time. In exchange for a cup of hot cocoa, I need an honest opinion on this website."

"Deal." Megan removed her coat and hung it on a peg, along with her scarf. "Nancy designs websites for the local businesses in Cardin."

They gathered around the computer. Onscreen, images of coffee beans and scrumptious-looking desserts scrolled against a background with a script logo.

"Oh, this is for the Wake Up Cafe. I keep meaning to go down there and visit with Rosa and her mother." Megan had been lying low since many townsfolk were upset about the investigation. "The website looks amazing, Nancy."

"You don't think it's too dark?"

"Not at all," Grace replied. "You've balanced it well with the logo colors and the images. Megan and I should hire you to update our site."

Nancy blushed and handed them each a steaming mug of cocoa topped with tiny marshmallows. "Of course, I'd love to it. Anytime."

"She's so sweet," Grace said as they walked through the living room toward the office. She took a sip from her mug and her eyes widened. "And this has to be the best hot chocolate I've ever had. I might never leave here."

"You and Archimedes both." Megan paused to run a hand over June's tabby cat. He'd taken over the recliner in front of the fireplace and was living his best life. "Nancy and Hank are both fantastic. I was nervous about staying here with them, considering a lunatic attacked me and burned my aunt's house down, but they insisted."

"They care about you. And speaking of people who care about you, how are things with Luke?"

"Nice try there, counselor. I see what you did with that transition."

"Thank goodness, because it wasn't all that smooth." Grace chuckled. "I can see there are feelings between you and Luke. It's as plain as the noses on your faces and obvious to anyone with eyeballs."

Megan's cheeks grew warm. She wasn't going there.

"Things between us are fine. Luke's taking the case seriously and looking at every angle." She pointed to the binder on the table in the office. "That one is yours. It's a copy of the entire case file. At least, everything we've been able to find."

Grace opened it and her expression grew solemn. "Is this Franny?"

"Yeah."

The young woman was front and center in the photograph. Her hair was cut in a pixie style, accenting her gorgeous cheekbones and beautiful eyes. Every time she looked at it, Megan's heart twisted painfully.

"It was taken on the day of her murder, at her birthday party." She swallowed hard. "She didn't deserve what happened to her, Grace."

"No. But we'll fight for her. We'll catch the person responsible."

"What if we can't? You and I have been through this before with other cases. The burden of proof to overturn a conviction is high. If the courts are convinced Wade is the killer, then how can we bring the real one to justice?" Megan sat her cocoa down on the table. "I want to believe things will work out, but I'm terrified they won't."

"That's where faith comes in." Grace touched the cross hanging from her necklace. "We do our very best and then we give the rest to God."

"I don't know if I can. So many bad things have happened—my parents' death, Franny's murder, my aunt's accident, Wade's conviction—I just can't see where having faith has helped. It feels...random."

"God doesn't promise bad things won't happen. He only promises to be with us when they do. It can feel like things happen without a reason, but our perspective is limited and judgments based on it don't help."

Grace's words struck a chord deep inside her, in a part of her heart she'd been ignoring for a long time. Like with Luke, Megan had closed off her relationship with God after Wade's arrest. She'd been holding on to the hurt and the anger. But it was time for a change.

Megan took a deep breath. "I don't know how to take the first step."

"Let's start with prayer." Grace held out her hands for Megan to take. "And see where that gets us."

Luke's truck bounced over a cattle guard as he entered the Dickersons' ranch. He turned to the right and headed down to the foreman's house, parking next to the old-fashioned windmill.

Chad was already outside. In one hand, he wielded a chainsaw running on idle. The other twirled a glass of whiskey. His shaggy hair was tucked underneath a dusty ball cap, the bill frayed at the corner, and he wore a pair of work jeans and a flannel shirt.

Luke came to a stop a safe distance away. "It's not a good idea to mix a chainsaw with alcohol."

"What's it to you?"

He shrugged. "It would be nice if emergency services didn't have to come out here because you cut your foot off."

Chad laughed. "Ain't happened yet."

He set the glass down on the porch railing, revved up the saw, and chopped through the block of wood. Sawdust flew and Luke was forced to take a few steps back. The scar along Chad's face caught the light. He'd been favored to win Nationals until his accident. The bull broke his femur and his arm, gave him a concussion severe enough to cause traumatic brain injury, and ruined Chad's chances of the fame he so desperately craved.

He released the power button on the chainsaw, and the decibel level lowered as the motor drifted into idle.

"I was wondering how long it would take before you came around, Tatum. News travels fast in Cardin, and rumor has it you're trying to get my sister's murderer out of prison."

"No, I'm trying to find out who attempted to kill June and Megan. Where were you this past Saturday from six in the morning till noon?"

The attack on Megan had happened around eight, but Luke wanted to make sure he covered a wider time frame.

Chad swirled the whiskey in his glass. "I was here."

"What were you doing?"

"I can't say I recall." His lips spread into a slow grin. "The doctors told me the injury to my brain could make it hard to remember things."

The little punk was getting a kick out of this. Luke's fingers twitched. He abhorred violence, but his patience was thin with bullies and those that took enjoyment from others' pain.

Chad lifted the whiskey glass and took a long drink.

"Maybe you should ask my dad. He might remember better." His smug smile widened, and he pointed to something behind Luke. "There he is now. You can ask him yourself."

A four wheeler kicked up dust as it came to a screeching stop. Heath Dickerson climbed off. His snakeskin boots matched the giant belt buckle at his waist, and the bolo around his neck swayed with every step.

He glared at his son, who was still holding the alcohol and the idling chainsaw. "Turn that contraption off."

Chad obliged and promptly drained the last of his drink. The ice clicked against the glass.

Heath swung his glare to Luke. Crow's-feet gathered at the edges of his eyes and grooved lines bracketed his hard mouth. "What are you doing here?"

"He's questioning me about June's accident and the fire at her house." Chad smirked. "Apparently, I'm a suspect."

"My son had nothing to do with that. He was with me." Heath's jaw tightened. "You have some nerve, Tatum. Dan called and said you might be coming by, pointing fingers and asking us questions."

Luke kept his tone casual, even as his stomach sank to his feet. His worst suspicions about the chief deputy were coming to fruition. "I'm not pointing fingers. I'm running an investigation."

"What a load of baloney." Chad rolled his eyes. "Megan's got you running around doing her dirty work. Is the bedroom action really that good, Tatum?"

Luke stiffened. It took every ounce of his willpower

and training to keep from crossing the yard and punching Chad in the face.

"Son, get in the house," Heath snapped. "Now."

The younger Dickerson swaggered up the porch steps. The screen door slammed shut, but Luke could still feel the weight of Chad's gaze on the back of his neck.

"If you need to talk to Chad or any of our employees"—Heath reached into his pocket and pulled out a business card—"call our attorney and set up an appointment."

"My investigation would go a lot faster if I had your cooperation."

"I didn't fall off the turnip truck yesterday, Tatum. I know exactly where you're going with this, and you aren't going to pin these attacks on my son. Nor am I going to allow you to sow the seeds of doubt about Wade's guilt."

Heath bared his teeth and his expression grew dark. "That man murdered my little girl, and while there is breath still left in my body, he's staying in prison to rot."

Luke's pulse kicked up a notch. Did he suspect the wrong Dickerson? Chad had made threats against Megan and June in the past, but Heath had his own axe to grind with the Hunt family.

Was it possible they were working together?

Right now, he didn't have enough evidence either way. He plucked the business card from Heath's outstretched hand. "I'll be in touch."

"I know you plan on taking over your stepfather's ranch and making Cardin your permanent home. It'll be hard to find another job in this county should you ruin the good thing you have going here." The older man stepped closer, dropping his voice. "Don't risk your career, Luke. She ain't worth it."

Like father, like son. Chad had tried the same tactic in the sheriff's office and the innuendo was getting on Luke's last nerve. "I'm a state officer. I'd be careful about making threats."

The corners of Heath's mouth lifted, but he didn't back up. "I'm merely giving you a friendly piece of advice. You'd be wise to heed it."

Luke met his gaze. "Did you know Franny was considering marrying Skeeter?"

The question was designed to catch Heath off guard, but not one flicker of surprise flashed in his expression.

"That's a lie." Heath's jaw clenched and his eyes narrowed. "My daughter made a mistake by getting involved with that nobody, but she saw the error of her ways. I won't listen to anyone speak badly of her."

"I mean no disrespect."

"No, I suppose you don't." Heath clapped a hand on his shoulder, the force of the slap a little too hard to be considered friendly. "But you do answer to God. Let my daughter lie in peace, Luke. It's all we have left."

He dropped his hand from Luke's shoulder and climbed the porch steps to the foreman's house.

"Oh, and one more thing, Luke. It might be a good idea for Megan to go back home. Now that June's house is gone and her business along with it, she might want to join her niece in Houston." Heath opened the screen door. "I'm sure once both women leave town, they'll be safe."

The man disappeared inside. Luke marched to his vehicle and got in, glancing at the house through his windshield. A curtain in the kitchen window fluttered. A pale face appeared, the sunlight winking off a silver necklace.

Karen Dickerson, Franny's mother.

Luke raised a hand, but before he got it halfway up, the curtain fluttered again, and she was gone.

THIRTEEN

Two days later, Megan tapped a marker against the palm of her hand and studied the whiteboard in Luke's home office. She'd made notes about Franny's murder, her aunt's accident, and the fire. Photographs of the scenes were held in place by magnets. A list of questions she couldn't answer were written on the far right side.

"I have a theory about how Franny's killer arranged to frame Wade," Megan said. "But not a lot of evidence to support it."

Luke frowned and leaned back in his chair. "Let me hear it anyway."

"At some point during the party, the killer stole Wade's phone and hid it. We know from Kyle that someone was with Franny. Either the killer returned to the house—like Wade did—or he never left."

She pointed to a photo of the lake house. "There's a back road that runs along the lake. If the killer thought ahead, he would've parked on this dirt path hidden in the woods. That way, it looks like everyone has left, but actually hasn't."

"Investigators looked at that road, but there had been a heavy downpour, so any tires tracks would've been washed away." He nodded. "Okay, I'm with you so far."

"He's someone Franny knows. Maybe even trusts. He offers to help her clean up since the party left a mess."

Megan pointed to the crime-scene photos. Several trash bags were open and placed in strategic areas around the downstairs. Paper plates and plastic cups spilled out.

"While picking up, the killer finds"—she used air quotes around finds—"Wade's cell phone in the couch and Franny calls Kyle. Arrangements are made for my brother to get his phone. At this point, the killer knows he's on his way, and he shoots Franny."

She paused, gripping the whiteboard marker tighter in her hand. Franny hadn't deserved what happened to her. *Lord, help me bring her killer to justice.*

She took a deep breath. "Wade comes into the house and sees Franny on the living room floor. He grabs his cell phone from the table in the entryway and bolts. My suspicion is the killer hadn't anticipated him doing that. I believe he thought Wade would call the police and therefore become the number-one suspect."

"When that doesn't happen, the blackmail starts." Luke was quiet for a long moment, his gaze flickering over the whiteboard. "It's a good theory, except it doesn't fit with the one motive we have. Neither Heath nor Chad were at the party that night. If Franny was killed over her relationship with Skeeter by one of her family members, then how did they arrange for Wade's cell phone to be taken?"

Megan bit her lip. "Maybe we're dealing with two people? Or our motive is wrong. Franny's death may have nothing to do with Skeeter at all. It would help if we could figure out what evidence June had uncovered."

Her hand drifted to the key hanging on a chain around her neck. Luke had made copies of the unidentified key from June's key ring, and they each had one. They still had no idea what it went to.

"Franny's missing journal is important," she continued. "Her friends confirmed she was tight-lipped about any problems she was going through, just as Wade told us. It makes sense she would use the journal as an outlet, but if that's what my aunt uncovered, I have no idea how."

"It's possible the evidence isn't something tangible, but it's a person. Like the woman who called you."

"Do you still think it could be Karen Dickerson?"

He shrugged. "The alibis Heath and Chad provided are weak. The foreman and a couple of ranch hands saw them on the days in question but were vague about the time."

"Even if they had a solid alibi, it doesn't rule them out since we could be looking at two people." She eyed the whiteboard. "And what about the missing evidence? It can't be a coincidence the box that disappeared contained several important interviews."

He smacked the table. "It's been days, and I feel like we are right where we started with this investigation."

"You're doing everything you can." She slid into the chair next to him and placed a hand on his arm. "That's all anyone can ask."

"It doesn't feel like enough. I want to catch this guy, Megs."

Something twisted perilously close to her heart. Hadn't she had a very similar conversation with Grace?

Luke's gaze lifted to meet hers. The sunlight coming in through the window played with his chiseled features, and her breath caught. There was pain swimming in the deep blue of his eyes, one she'd helped put there with her words and her actions.

"You didn't do anything wrong, Luke. I shouldn't have blamed you for Wade's conviction. None of this is your fault. Or mine. It's not even my brother's, although he made some big mistakes. It was easier to be angry with you than to accept it wasn't any one person's fault. It was a perfect storm of decisions and choices that led us here."

"Do you really believe that?"

"One hundred percent. There's only one person to blame for Franny's murder and that's her killer."

His hand slid over hers and warmth replaced the worry in his eyes. Butterflies fluttered in her stomach.

"Thank you, Megs. I needed the reminder." Luke rose and tugged on her hand to encourage her out of the chair. "Come on. We've been at this nonstop for hours. Let's take a break and clear our heads with a horseback ride."

She hesitated, but stealing thirty minutes away was too tempting to turn down. The last couple of days had consisted of reading Franny's case file and sitting by June's bedside.

They bundled in jackets, and Luke led Megan across the yard. The sunshine offset the chill in the air, and a flock of birds soared overhead. Inside the barn, a horse stuck her neck out and nickered.

Megan's mouth dropped open. "Fiona?"

She hurried down the aisle until she was standing in front of the animal. The distinct blaze down the horse's nose was as familiar to Megan as her own foot.

"It is you." She lifted her hand for the horse to smell before proceeding to stroke her. "What are you doing here, girl?"

"I bought her," Luke said. "I have Remnant too. He's down that way."

She glanced behind her and caught sight of the beautiful black bay. A warmth spread through her chest.

"I had no idea... I can't believe my aunt sold them to you."

"She didn't know. At least, not till after. I bought them at the rodeo auction." He shrugged. "I couldn't stand the thought of them going to strangers."

His image blurred as tears flooded her eyes. She flung her arms around his neck and hugged him.

"Thank you, Luke."

Megan's heart skittered when his hand cupped the back of her head, his fingers dipping into the strands of her hair. His scent and warmth surrounded her, his arm encircling her waist and holding her close. He was hard muscle and rough edges, all masculine, and a direct contrast to her soft curves.

His phone trilled and Megan jumped back. Cold air replaced the heat of his body, and she shivered. Luke pulled the phone from his belt. Creases formed between his brows and he jabbed the reject button.

"Everything okay?" she asked.

"It's fine."

That funny note was in his voice again. Luke almost always answered his phone, so why...

Her chest tightened as the most obvious answer popped into her mind. She backed up toward the barn entrance. "Seriously, I can give you a few minutes. I mean, it's completely fine if you have a girlfriend you need to talk to."

"Megs."

"Don't avoid answering her call on my account... There's no reason to..."

A blush heated her cheeks, and she was rambling but couldn't stop. The image of Luke tangled up in another woman's arms, kissing her, flashed before Megan's eyes. A small surge of panic sent her heart racing.

He stepped toward her. "Megs—"

"We're both adults, and it's been a long time since we broke up. It makes sense that you—"

"Megs, for heaven's sake, let me talk. It's not my girlfriend. It's my dad."

She froze, certain she'd heard him wrong. "What?"

"The phone calls. The person I keep avoiding. It's not my girlfriend." He took a deep breath. "It's my dad."

———

Luke mentally kicked himself the entire time they prepared the horses for riding. He shouldn't have told her about his dad, but the look on her face when she realized he might have a girlfriend...it'd sucker punched him while he was still reeling from their hug. Things were shifting between them, and he didn't have the strength to keep fighting it.

Megan brought Fiona next to his horse, Domino, as they rode across the property toward the woods along the outer edge.

"Okay, Luke." She held the reins with one hand and waved the other in a circular motion. "Let's have it. What's going on with your dad?"

"Never mind," he responded. She had enough problems on her plate without adding his. "Forget I said anything."

"Uhhh, no. You cannot drop a bombshell like that and then just pretend it didn't happen. Something is bothering you, so just spill it." Her mouth quirked up. "Being a sounding board is the least I can do. You did save my life the other day."

"I didn't know we were keeping score."

"Competitiveness is a Hunt family trait, right behind stubbornness and the ridiculously huge gap between our toes."

He chuckled. They entered the cool confines of the forest. Sunlight dappled on the ground, and the trail was wide enough their horses could walk side by side.

"There isn't much to tell, Megs. My dad moved nearby about six months ago. He wants to reconcile."

"And you don't?"

He shrugged. "I've lived a long time without him, and it's not like I'm a kid anymore. I don't need him. I consider Hank my real dad, anyway. He's the one who raised me."

"The last time you saw Patrick, you were fifteen, right?"

He nodded. Luke had never told Megan the details about his father, preferring to keep it all behind him. But his past was colliding with his present, brought into focus by his father's appearance in town and his phone calls, and Luke couldn't keep ignoring it forever.

"Patrick signed the paperwork terminating his parental rights at the lawyer's office so Hank could adopt me. I refused to see him when that happened, so only my mom and Hank went. But somehow Patrick found out when the adoption was going before the judge and he showed up at the courthouse. He was drunk and said awful things. Stuff about how I'd betrayed him and that he disowned me."

Domino tossed his head and Luke realized he was gripping the reins. He took a deep breath and forced his muscles to relax.

"I should've kept quiet, but I had a lot of anger built up toward him. My dad hadn't been sober since I was six.

I mean, he tried rehab, but it never stuck. There were a lot of promises broken. Times he was supposed to show up and didn't. Or he would come drunk. Anyway, I couldn't hold back anymore. I said some bad things, and it got heated. We ended up in a fistfight right there in the courtroom."

Somewhere overhead a hawk cried out and took flight. The cold air had put color in Megan's cheeks, and her body moved with Fiona's, a natural extension of the horse. They'd gone deeper into the forest than Luke realized. He cleared his mind, listening, but the only sounds were the clopping of the horse hooves and the rushing of the water from the nearby creek.

"Shortly after the courthouse fight, my dad was convicted of a second DUI and disappeared. That is, until he showed up in Cardin."

"No wonder you're worried about letting him back into your life." She was quiet for a moment. "Fifteen years is a long time, Luke. Maybe he's changed. He says he's sober, right?"

"Yes, but... I dunno, Megs. He hasn't been a part of my life for a long time. And for most of my childhood, when he was involved, it wasn't good."

"True, but you and I are cut from the same cloth. We believe in the goodness of people and in their ability to change. Your dad calls and you don't answer, but you also don't tell him to stop. Maybe a part of you is hoping there's a chance to heal things."

Luke opened his mouth to deny it but choked on the words. There was a thread of truth to what she'd said.

Still, there was so much hurt between him and his father, he couldn't see a path through it.

There was parting in the trees, revealing a small clearing and the creek. The air was scented faintly with the water, clean and crisp.

"Can we rest for a bit?" Megan pulled her horse to a stop and dismounted. "I haven't ridden in a long time and my body is reminding me of that."

"Sure." He dismounted Domino and let the reins fall to the ground. "Do you miss it? Riding?"

"I do. I didn't realize how much until now." Picking up a rock, she sent it skipping over the water. It jumped twice before plopping into the creek. "Work has taken over my life in the last few years. Maybe when every-thing is settled, I'll figure out a way to balance things better."

"What about dating?" He peeked at her out of the corner of his eye. "Are you seeing anyone?"

"Uhhh, no." She shoved her hands into the pockets of her jacket. "Dating hasn't been high on my priority list."

He let out the breath he was holding. Luke picked up a rock and sent it sailing through the air. It skipped three times across water before landing in the creek.

"Show off." She pushed him lightly, her face split into a wide grin. "You just can't let me get a win."

"You would hate it if I didn't challenge—"

She put a finger to her lips and pointed into the trees. "Look."

He followed the line of her finger. Two deer stepped from the camouflage of the forest into the clearing. They paused, but Luke and Megan were downwind. With graceful steps, they approached the creek to drink.

She watched them with an enraptured look on her face. "I'd forgotten how magical this place could be."

The wind rustled her hair, sending strands of it into her face. Without thinking, Luke reached up and pushed them back. The touch was featherlight, barely more than a brush of his fingers against her face, and yet it quickened his heartbeat.

Their eyes snagged and Megan's breath hitched. She shifted, the movement nearly indecipherable, except his fingers were still tangled in the strands of her hair, still grazing her cheek, and he felt it. Longing settled in Luke's gut, making him ache for more than was reasonable.

His gaze dropped to her mouth. He leaned closer.

A red laser light flashed on her cheek. Luke spun, taking Megan with him. A bullet whistled right past his ear and thudded into the dirt where Megan had been just a breath before. The horses bolted as the crack of a rifle shot echoed.

"Run," Luke yelled.

He pushed Megan toward the trees, using his body to provide cover. His heart pounded in his ears. Megan's shoes lost traction against the leaves and grass. She stumbled.

Another whistle and a thud as a bullet lodged itself in the ground nearby. Luke wrapped his arm around her waist and dove behind two large pines and an array of bushes.

He pulled his weapon while scanning her body for possible injuries. "You hit?"

"I'm fine." Her breaths were coming in pants. "You?"

"Still in one piece."

Thank you, Lord.

Luke reached down and pulled his clutch piece from a specially sewn pocket in his boot. "Do you still know how to shoot?"

She nodded. "I've kept up with the skills June taught me."

He handed the gun to her before peeking around the tree. Everything had gone still and quiet.

Holding his breath, he scanned the direction the bullets had come from. Bushes rustled on the other side of the creek. He glimpsed someone in camouflage running, heading for the trail leading to the road.

"Stay here and call 911. I'm going after him."

Luke bolted through the underbrush along the creek bed. His pulse skyrocketed as he left the safety of the trees and sprinted through the water, soaking the bottom of his jeans. The shooter had a decent lead, but Luke knew these woods like the back of his hand. He took a shortcut and spotted a figure in full camouflage up ahead.

"Police! Freeze!"

The shooter didn't stop. Luke put all his focus into closing the gap between them. His boots skidded on dried pine needles and sweat coated his back.

The man spun, lifting his weapon, and Luke had seconds to dive for cover. Bark exploded as bullets impacted the tree above him. He gritted his teeth, the desire to give chase fighting with his common sense. The shooter had a rifle. Luke only had a handgun, and while he was an excellent shot, he was severely disadvantaged.

The rev of an engine sent him scrambling. He raced toward the sound. A dark pickup truck, dirt obscuring its plates, flew down the main trail to the road. The vehicle disappeared around a corner and was swallowed up by the trees.

FOURTEEN

Dan flipped his notepad closed and tucked it and a pen back into the front pocket of his uniform. "Sounds like someone was hunting deer out of season."

Megan's mouth dropped open and heat flooded her cheeks. "You have got to be kidding me."

Wind moved through the forest, rustling the leaves, but Dan's hair didn't flutter. The strands were loaded down with so much product, it appeared painted in place.

The chief deputy, along with Sheriff Franklin, arrived shortly after responding deputies. Two hours had gone by since the shooting, but a mixture of lawmen—troopers and deputies—still worked the scene around them.

"He was aiming for Megan," Luke growled. "Not the deer. And he used a laser scope. It's hard to justify that as a mistake."

"You'd be surprised. Last year, a poacher nearly took

out Old Man McGregor's dog using a laser scope." Dan smirked, pulling his e-cigarette out of his pocket. "If someone wanted to kill you, this seems like a hard way to do it. How did the shooter know ya'll were out here?"

"Spyware can be installed remotely on a phone to track someone."

Luke and Megan had turned off their cells. An analyst was on his way to the ranch to check the devices for any spying software.

"If you find it, then we can reevaluate." Dan took a drag of his e-cigarette and blew out cherry-scented smoke. "In my experience, if it walks like a duck and quacks like a duck, it's a duck."

Megan gritted her teeth together, the ache in her jaw spreading into her scalp. She didn't know if the chief deputy was merely negligent or purposefully muddying the waters, but either way, he was dangerous.

Sheriff Franklin came out of the woods and approached. Judging from his reddened eyes and chapped upper lip, the sheriff was fighting off a nasty cold. Megan reached into her jacket pocket and pulled out a packet of aspirin. She'd been carrying them around since her fall down the stairs.

"Sheriff?" She extended her hand, offering the medication.

He smiled, causing his jowls to stretch, and took the packet. "Thanks. Woke up this morning feeling like I'd been hit by a dump truck."

Sheriff Franklin sniffed and turned to Dan. "I think

we're almost done here. Can you coordinate the deputies and start putting them back on patrol?"

"Sure thing." Dan ambled off, smoke trailing behind him, and greeted a deputy standing near the crime-scene tape with a clap on the back. The two men talked for a moment before laughing.

"Dan thinks this was someone hunting out of season," Luke said.

"On its own, I might agree, but with everything else that's been going on...something about this ain't sitting right." The sheriff pulled a handkerchief out of his pocket and swiped it under his nose. His expression grew dark. "I don't like that the perpetrator shot at you, Luke, when you were in pursuit."

Megan flinched. The moments between hearing the rifle shots and Luke reappearing in the clearing had been the longest and worst of her life. Her instincts had been to go after him, to help, but logic kept her feet in place. Sneaking through the forest could've put them both in more danger. Instead, she'd closed her eyes and prayed.

"Chad Dickerson drives a black F-150," Luke pointed out.

"So does half the county." Sheriff Franklin tucked his handkerchief back in the pocket of his uniform. "Still, I don't like this cloud hanging over the family. Nor do I like anyone taking potshots at lawmen in my county. I'm gonna talk to Heath myself, convince them to come in for an interview. In the meantime, ya'll keep me informed of anything you uncover."

He tipped his hat to Megan and patted Luke on the back before heading down the trail toward the road.

Megan sighed. "It's a shame Sheriff Franklin's retiring. There's no telling what will happen once Dan is in charge."

Luke's jaw tightened. "One problem at a time, Megs."

"Hey, Greg's at your house and set up to check your phones." Weston approached and handed his keys to Luke. "Here, take my truck. I'll catch a ride with one of the troopers once the forensics team is done to pick it up."

They took the trail through the woods to the road where the vehicles were parked, each lost in their own thoughts. Megan wanted to focus on the case, but the echo of the gunshot kept reverberating in her head. She reached for Luke's hand, interlacing her fingers with his. He pulled her closer to his side and squeezed her hand gently.

When they located Weston's truck, Luke opened the passenger-side door for her. Megan's heart sprinted as her gaze drifted to his lips. It wasn't logical—she would end up brokenhearted—but she couldn't deny her feelings. They'd almost kissed down by the creek before the attack. By the grace of God, they'd survived the shooting, and Megan wasn't going to waste the blessing.

She rose up on her tiptoes and brushed her mouth against Luke's. A simple kiss, gentle and light, but electricity jolted straight through her. When she pulled back, he looked stunned.

"What was that for?"

"For saving my life." She lightly smacked his chest

with the back of her hand. It was like hitting a boulder. "And that's for scaring me half to death. You aren't bullet-proof, you know."

He chuckled, his gaze dropping to her mouth. "I'll try to remember that next time."

"See that you do."

He cupped her face, sending a wave of heat through her body. His breath wafted over her lips moments before his mouth closed over hers. She melted against him, losing herself in the sensation of the moment, and everything else drifted away. All that remained was the tender way he touched her, the rapid beat of her heart, the swell of long-buried emotions breaking free.

When the kiss ended, they were both breathless.

"Come on," Luke said, brushing his thumb gently across her lower lip. "Let's get home. The analyst is waiting for us."

An hour later, Megan studied the whiteboard in Luke's office. It was a giant jigsaw puzzle of suspects and evidence. She knew the answers were there, but plucking out the right ones was hard. If there was any doubt someone was trying to prevent them from getting to the truth, that was laid to rest with today's attack.

Nearby, Luke and the analyst, Greg, scanned her cell phone for spyware. Both of Luke's cells—one business, one personal—had already been cleared. The two men chatted while they talked, their voices a low murmur against the backdrop of Megan's thoughts.

Who killed you, Franny? And why?

"This phone is clean too," Greg announced, straightening his wire-rim glasses. "There's no spy software on any of your devices."

"Are you sure?" Luke rocked back on his heels. "I can't believe this was a random attack."

"How many people knew you were going riding?" Greg asked. "Is it possible someone on your staff alerted the shooter?"

"No. I suppose a worker could've come back and found the stalls empty, but that wouldn't have told them where we were going to be. I have security on the farm, but it only extends to the fence line and doesn't include the woods."

The memory of Dan's smirk flashed in Megan's mind. His arrogance got under her skin, and he'd been so sure they wouldn't find anything on the phones. She fingered her shirt. Could there be a GPS tracker in their clothes or...

She smacked her forehead. "Of course. I know how he tracked us."

She spun on her heel and walked to the barn. Luke followed, as did Greg.

The horses, startled by the gunshots, had run straight home. They were nestled in their stalls and she patted Fiona on her way to the tack room.

"I haven't been riding in Houston, but I went to the Livestock Show and Rodeo every year. Saddle theft is a serious problem." Megan searched her saddle and quickly located the hidden tracker. "They're designed to turn on when the saddle is moved and they provide GPS coordinates."

Luke's jaw tightened and his gaze narrowed. "So much for Dan's theory that we were in the wrong place at the wrong time."

Together, they searched the other saddles. The only ones with trackers were the three brought from June's property.

Luke turned to Greg. "Can this be traced back to the owner?"

"Possibly. Let me run inside and do a quick search on the manufacturer."

He left, and Luke prowled the tack room. His lips flattened into a hard line and his hands balled into fists.

"How long could those trackers have been on the saddles?" he asked.

"The battery can last for more than a month before needing to be recharged. It's possible the killer initially put it for my aunt, but I don't think so."

"Neither do I. The message spray-painted on June's barn wall was for our benefit. If you were worried someone had broken into the barn, you'd want to keep the saddles safe."

"I'd bring them here, just like I did with Cinnamon." She caught on to the train of his thought. "It was only a matter of time before I went riding, and naturally, I would use a saddle I was familiar with."

He nodded. "You heard Dan. Poachers are often a

problem in rural areas, which is what the shooter was counting on. He wanted to disguise our murders as a hunting accident gone wrong."

Her mind spun, whirling with information she'd gathered about the case so far. Her heart skipped a beat.

"Luke, someone else connected to this case was killed in a similar way."

He paused midstep, his eyes widening. "Franny's boyfriend, Skeeter McIntyre."

"Wow. Now Skeeter's death could be a part of this." Brent rubbed a hand over his bald head. His wedding ring winked in the fluorescent light. "Why is it every time I talk to you, this case gets weirder and weirder?"

Luke leaned against the hospital wall and sighed. Exhaustion bit into him. Across the hall, the door to June's room was cocked open. Megan was arranging sunflowers in a vase, and she appeared to be having a conversation with her unconscious aunt. A phone rang at the nurse's station.

"Trust me, I wish it was a lot easier," Luke said. "What do you think? Sound similar?"

"Could be. Skeeter wasn't shot in our county, but the next one over. From what I understand, he was hunting with a group of friends and was killed by a stray bullet. Skeeter wasn't wearing a reflective vest at the time, and his friends were cleared of any wrongdoing. The investigators chalked it up to a hunting accident."

It wasn't exactly the same setup as the shooting today, but it was close enough to send chills down Luke's spine.

Brent leaned a shoulder against the wall. "So what happens now? Are you going to compare the bullets and casings recovered from both scenes?"

"Yep. If we're lucky, and the cases are connected, the shooter used the same gun."

"Man, poor Megs. That must've been terrifying." Brent sent him a knowing gaze. "For you too."

Luke's gaze drifted again toward June's room. Megan was now perched on the edge of the bed, reading from the Bible, her silky hair hiding her exquisite features. This morning's shooting cemented the killer would stop at nothing to silence her. It hurt to breathe when he thought about how close he'd come to losing her.

"He's not going to stop until they're dead," Luke said, his worst fears clawing at his insides. "The only way to protect them is to solve this case."

"I should've checked those saddles over. I didn't even think—"

"There was no way for you to know, Brent. Don't beat yourself up about it." He paused. "How's your mom doing?"

Brent hadn't been one of the responding deputies at the scene because he'd been at the oncologist with his mother.

He frowned. "She's responding to the chemo, and they're talking about surgery again now that the tumor has shrunk."

"That's good, right?"

"It is." Brent sighed. "But the insurance company will fight it, I'm sure. They've got me buried in paperwork and bills."

"If there's anything you need, all you have to do is ask. Anything. Even money."

"I know. Thanks, man." He pushed off from the wall and adjusted his duty belt. "I'd better get a move on. I'm on patrol, and I've been here a while. Thanks again, and anything you need, let me know."

"Will do."

When he disappeared down the hall, Luke rested his head back and sent his gaze skyward.

Lord, help Brent and his mom. Cancer's a hard thing. Also, Lord, please give Megan comfort and help June heal. Give me the strength to find this killer and protect the innocent.

Luke continued his conversation with God while he waited. There was so much going on, not just with the case but also in his personal life. He didn't know where the relationship with Megan was going. He cared about her, but could they really get beyond their past? Wouldn't his actions—keeping the truth of Wade's struggles from her and his role in handing over the evidence to the sheriff—always linger between them?

In his mind, the answers were obvious. Yes. His own relationship with his father was proof that second chances never provided a fresh slate. But his heart...his heart longed to ignore his common sense.

Megan emerged from the hospital room. Her shoulders were curved inward, and she looked pale. Luke closed the distance between them and pulled her into his arms. There wasn't much he could do to ease her burden, except provide comfort and prayers. He intended to do both.

She rested her head against his chest and sighed. "I can't control it, but I want to will her into getting well. Does that sound strange?"

"No. You're a fixer. You see something wrong and you want to make it better. It's frustrating when you can't. I struggle with the same thing. But, Megs, you're doing everything you can."

"I know. The rest is up to God." She tightened her arms around his waist. "If I haven't said it enough, thank you. I don't know how I would've gotten through all of this without you."

The woman made him feel ten feet tall. If he could prevent an ounce of hurt coming her direction, he would do it.

"I'm your friend. It's my job to hold you up." He shifted, reaching into the pocket of his jacket, and pulled out a package of jelly beans. "And provide comfort snacks."

Her eyes lit up, just as he'd hoped, and she surprised him with a quick kiss. Luke's heart took off like a racehorse. He was tempted to lean in for another, but they were standing in the middle of the hospital hallway.

She narrowed her gaze at him, and her gorgeous mouth twitched. "Did you buy these for me, or were you craving the red ones and I'm the only person you know who will eat the rest?"

He groaned. "You always uncover my plan."

They both laughed, and she opened the package. "We make a good team, Luke."

"We do, Megs. We definitely do."

He wrapped an arm around her neck and snuck a red jelly bean out of her bag. She protested and slapped his hand away but was grinning from ear to ear. The elevator ride was short, and as they approached the main exit, Luke swept his gaze over the parking lot. It was late and darkness had fallen swiftly.

Megan's hand wrapped around his elbow, and she slid up close to him. "What is it?"

"Nothing. Just being cautious. Keep holding on to me and let's move quickly to the vehicle."

Several of the parking-lot lights were out, casting deeper shadows in certain areas. Luke had specifically parked close to the front. As they passed a couple on the sidewalk, he gave them a nod of his head. Cold wind rattled the awning.

He halted. The hair on the back of his neck rose, and he scanned the parking lot again. There. A man sitting in a truck. Barely more than a shadow, but he was there. Luke's fingers drifted toward his gun.

The driver must've realized he'd been made because the truck's engine revved and the headlights flipped on. No, not headlights. His brights. They were designed to blind Luke, but he'd anticipated the action and averted his gaze in time. He pushed Megan behind him, keeping his body between her and the truck, even as his feet propelled them backward toward the safety of the hospital.

What was the plan? To run over them? Or to shoot at them?

Luke kept his breathing steady as he unsnapped his holster. His gaze flickered from the truck to assess the parking lot in quick snaps. No one else was there, thank goodness. He didn't want innocent bystanders caught in the middle.

Tires squealed as the truck bolted out of the parking spot. It was black. Clean, but the same style and design as the one that the shooter had used this morning. Luke noted the license plate and looked for any decals.

His heart jumped as the truck whipped through the parking lot. He pushed Megan harder toward the corner of the building and they took cover as the vehicle passed them. Luke got a clear view of the driver.

Chad Dickerson.

FIFTEEN

Every day since Megan had arrived in town, the need for her blood pulsed through him. He'd almost had it today.

Almost.

He parked the truck in the garage and went inside, shrugging off his jacket before pouring a glass of whiskey. The liquid burned a path down his throat. Alcohol numbed the urges and took off the edge. The rifle sat on the table, ready to be cleaned. His fingers followed the line of the barrel. The cool metal chilled his skin. Megan's face had been in his scope, his laser guiding the perfect path to take her out.

And then he'd missed.

His hand tightened around the glass, the jagged edges of the crystal biting into the soft flesh of his palm. Some of the best hunters in the world missed shots, but these stakes were so much higher. For the first time, he felt the nip of Lady Justice on his heels.

He shook, his body heat rising like a volcano, until he

screamed. The glass flew from his hand. It smashed against the wall and shattered into pieces. The cloying scent of alcohol filled the room.

He was not going to prison. Not now. Not ever.

He was a hunter. Deer. Humans. It was all the same. He took a shuddering breath. Sacrifices would have to be made, but there was a way to salvage this.

Next time, it would be a kill shot. Then he would have blood.

Luke's. Megan's.

And anyone else who threatened to get in his way.

SIXTEEN

The following morning, Luke parked his Suburban in the Dickersons' driveway and got out. Warm sunshine hit the back of his neck and the scent of freshly cut grass carried on the wind. He'd arrived a minute or two early for the interview with the family and their attorney, hoping Chad would already be there. Luck was with him because a black pickup sat three cars away. He'd have to pass it on the way to the front door.

He slowed his steps as he approached the vehicle. The chrome bumper gleamed, and a hunting decal decorated the back window on the driver's side. Luke closed his eyes, bringing up the image of the truck fleeing from the shooting yesterday. Had there been a decal in the back window? He couldn't be sure.

Luke circled the truck, peeking inside through the windows. It was an extended cab, fully decked out with a high-priced stereo system and leather seats. It was spotlessly clean. A gun rack was installed on the interior roof, but there were no weapons.

Sheriff Franklin drove up, his boots hitting the cement with a thump as he exited his vehicle. He raised a hand in greeting before sneezing.

"This stupid cold is gonna be the death of me."

They went up the walkway to the house together, and Luke rang the bell. Ed Rhodes, the Dickersons' family attorney, opened the door moments later. His comb-over was swirled low on his forehead and his eyes bulged behind his glasses, giving him a faint frog-like appearance.

The attorney escorted them inside to the living room. Half-drunk glasses of sweet tea sat on the coffee table next to a plate of cookies. Chad lounged in a leather armchair, an insolent expression on his face. His eyes were bloodshot, as though he'd been up late drinking, but he appeared sober at the moment.

Heath stood behind his son, his arms crossed over his chest.

Franny's mother, Karen, rose to greet them with a handshake. Slender with a pixie haircut, she was a mirror image of her late daughter.

"Can I get you gentleman any iced tea?" she asked. "Or some coffee?"

"They aren't houseguests, Karen," Heath snapped. "They're here to pin a murder on us."

Her complexion paled, and bit down on her lower lip.

Luke offered her a smile. "No, thank you, ma'am."

Sheriff Franklin removed his hat and set it on the

back of a chair. "We're not here to pin a murder on anyone."

"Well, you didn't come to sell us Girl Scout cookies." Heath rocked on the heels of his snakeskin boots. "Let's get to it."

"What were you doing at Memorial Hospital last night?" Luke asked, directing his question to Chad.

He smirked. "Getting stitches."

Chad unbuttoned the cuff of his shirt and lifted the sleeve, revealing a bandage on his forearm.

"A bull didn't want to move to his new pen." His grin widened. "Would you like to see the bill too?"

Luke kept his expression neutral, but Chad's smugness didn't sit well. It wasn't beyond the realm of possibility he'd been injured days ago.

"I would appreciate having a copy of the bill," Luke said. "Thank you for offering."

"Oh, come on," Heath exploded. "Are you kidding me? This is bordering on harassment, Sheriff."

Ed cleared his throat. "My clients are understandably upset. They've cooperated with the investigation and provided alibis for several days in question, including their daughter's own murder."

"I'd still like a copy of the hospital bill."

"You'll have it this afternoon." Ed straightened his pinky ring. "Anything else?"

"Actually, yes, there is." Luke kept his gaze on the Dickerson family. "Where were each of you on November 30th two years ago?"

Chad sat up straight. "That's the day Skeeter was shot."

"I'm going to object to this line of questioning," Ed said. "How can my clients remember where they were two years ago—?"

"That's all right," Heath interrupted. "We know where we were."

He stepped forward and placed a hand on his wife's shoulder. She flinched slightly before smoothing her expression into a carefully constructed mask.

"We were here, Ranger," Karen said. "That's my birthday, and I'd arranged a party for that evening. Heath and Chad were helping to set up the decorations and the outside tent for the festivities."

"The entire day?"

"Yes." She smiled, but the edges were tight. "I'm sure our foreman will confirm it for you. He was also helping."

The same foreman had provided alibis for both Chad and Heath for two other incidents—the hours before June's car accident and the day of Megan's attack. The man's word didn't mean much. Heath could've paid him off, but proving it would be difficult.

Heath released his wife's shoulder, and Karen took a deep breath. Luke's gut churned. He'd been around abused women enough times to recognize the subtle clues. Karen's voice was smooth and cultured. He tried to compare it to the woman calling to warn Megan, but like the decal on Chad's truck, he couldn't be sure.

Ed straightened his posture. "Why are you asking

about my clients' whereabouts on the day Skeeter was killed?"

Luke opened his mouth to give them a canned answer, but Sheriff Franklin cut him off.

"A ballistics analysis confirms the rifle used to shoot at Megan and Ranger Tatum yesterday was the same weapon used to kill Skeeter," he said. "Obviously, that changes the investigation."

Luke kept his posture relaxed and his attention on the family, but his mind was racing. Why would the sheriff have shared that information? It would've been far better to keep that fact out of the public domain.

"So Skeeter didn't die in a hunting accident?" Ed asked. "He was murdered?"

Karen's hands tightened in her lap, the knuckles turning white with the effort. Heath's gaze darted to his son. Chad lounged in the chair, the corners of his mouth tipped up.

Sheriff Franklin stepped forward. "Heath. Karen. I've been a friend of your family for a long time, and I hope I've earned your trust. If any of you know something about these incidents, now is the time to tell me." He paused. "I can help you, but I can only do that if you tell me the truth."

The room was as silent as a grave. Karen's face paled even more until she was almost translucent. Luke held his breath, the sheriff's motives in sharing the ballistic analysis becoming clear. He was applying pressure.

Heath jutted out his chin. "We don't know anything and we aren't involved."

"Then I'm sure you'd be happy to prove it," Luke said. "I'd like permission to examine the guns you own."

"Absolutely not." Ed puffed out his chest. "My clients have cooperated and provided their whereabouts for the times in question. There is no reason to drag them through a search of their personal property as well."

Every delay the family and their attorney put on his investigation only made Luke more suspicious of their involvement. He played the only card he had. "If you make me obtain a search warrant, I'll turn this into a media fanfare."

Ed didn't blink. "You don't have the probable cause necessary for a search warrant, Ranger Tatum."

"Not yet. But make no mistake, this isn't over. Not by a long shot."

Megan placed Skeeter's photograph next to Franny's on the whiteboard and took a giant step back. From his bed in the corner of the room, Jax sighed and rolled over. The dog had been with her all morning, sleeping, while she read Skeeter McIntyre's case file.

It hadn't helped. Megan hadn't uncovered any new threads to pull.

Jax lifted his head and gave a bark. Luke? Was he finally back? Megan's heart skipped a beat, and she turned, a smile hovering on her lips.

Weston appeared in the doorway.

She let out a whoosh of air, and her shoulders dropped. "Oh, hey."

"Ouch." He put a hand over his heart. "I've had prisoners give me a better greeting than that."

She laughed. "Sorry. I thought you were Luke. He went to interview the Dickersons this morning and hasn't come back yet. The suspense is torture."

"He invited me for lunch, so he should be back soon." Weston stepped farther into the room and eyed the board. "Anything interesting in Skeeter's case file? I've started it but haven't read the whole thing."

"You aren't missing much. The investigation focused on clearing the friends Skeeter had been hunting with. An attempt was made to locate any other hunters in the area, but the search was unsuccessful. It never occurred to the investigators to consider Skeeter's death was linked to Franny's."

Nancy poked her head in the office. "Hey, you two, Luke's back. He and Hank are already fixing plates, so if you want to grab some food, you'd better hurry."

"Oh, no, they better not." Weston bolted for the doorway, shouting, "I call dibs on the rolls."

Megan and Nancy followed, laughing. The scents of roasted chicken and melted cheese filled the kitchen. Spread across the long table was enough food for an army.

Luke grinned when he caught sight of Megan and gestured at a chair next to him.

"I fixed you a plate already," he said. "Otherwise,

there might not be anything left with this human garbage disposal over here."

Weston scooped green beans onto his plate. "Yeah, yeah. Like you and Hank don't eat like wildebeests."

Luke's stepfather grunted. "We live here."

Hank glared at Weston across the table as the younger man reached for the bread. "You take the last roll and I'll harm you, boy."

Weston's hand froze over the plate before he deliberately backed away. Megan and Luke shared a glance and smothered their chuckles. Hank might be retired, but the former Marine general could still stop a man in his tracks.

"No need to get cranky, Hank." Nancy shook her finger at her husband before patting Weston's shoulder. "There are plenty of rolls."

She pulled another set out of the oven. Once everyone was seated with their plates, they all joined hands and Hank blessed the food. During the meal, everyone chatted and laughed. It warmed Megan's heart. Her life in Houston felt far away and lonely. She had Grace, but that was it. She'd left Cardin and, in doing so, closed herself off to everything resembling home.

Luke caught her eye and the corners of his lips tilted up. Her breath hitched. Since their kiss, the feelings simmering below the surface became impossible to ignore. Learning about Luke's relationship with his father brought her own decision to bail on their relationship in stark clarity. Yes, he'd messed up by not telling her about Wade's drinking, but she'd exacerbated the situation by breaking things off without giving him a chance to explain. Was there a way for them both to fully move past the hurt? She didn't know, and with a killer breathing down their necks, it wasn't the right time to sort it out.

After lunch was finished, and the dishes done, Hank and Nancy went outside to tend to a sick horse. Luke took three cups down from the cabinet and Megan filled them with coffee. She frowned, watching the older couple cross the yard hand in hand.

"Luke, they'll be safe, right? On the property?"

"Yeah. Hank's staying with Mom, just in case, but they are keeping to the areas where we have the security system in place. Plus, I checked all the saddles. There aren't any other trackers." He glanced at Weston. "Speaking of which, any luck tracing the ones we recovered?"

"Dead end. They were bought using a shell corporation registered to the Caymans. It's impossible to trace beyond that. What about you, Luke? How did the interview with the Dickersons go?"

Luke shared the conversation and his observations, frustration bleeding into his voice. "The problem is, the attorney is right. We don't have enough probable cause to get a search warrant."

Weston nodded. "Now that Chad's aware we know Skeeter was murdered with the same weapon used to shoot at the two of you, chances are he'll get rid of the rifle."

"I know." Luke rubbed his chin. "I would've preferred to keep that information to myself, but Sheriff Franklin shared it."

Megan gripped her mug tighter. Why would the sheriff tell the Dickersons about a key piece of information? Was he protecting them? She hadn't been in the interview, so it was hard to judge his intentions.

"We know two of the incidents are linked because of the evidence." Luke took a sip of his coffee. "Same gun indicates the same killer."

"Agreed," Weston said. "The real question we need to figure out is—if Franny's murder is linked to Skeeter's —why did the killer wait so long?"

"He didn't want to attract attention. Killing Franny and then Skeeter back to back would've caught law enforcement's curiosity. By spacing the murders out over the course of a year and killing Skeeter in a different county, he reduces the likelihood of them being connected."

Megan nodded. "Different weapons too. Franny was shot with a handgun. Skeeter with a rifle. Add my brother's confession into the mix and there's very little chance anyone would've considered them linked."

"Except your aunt," Luke said. "June believed Wade was innocent from the get-go. She would've investigated Skeeter's death herself. Maybe that's what led her to find the evidence she called you about."

"I don't think so." She frowned. "I mean, I think June figured out they were connected, but Skeeter died two years ago. Unless some new fact has arisen in the case in the last couple of months, I can't see how that would've helped."

"I keep circling back to Chad. His alibis are weak and

he's the only suspect so far with a clear motive. He was angry with Franny and Skeeter over their relationship. He kills his sister and frames Wade. Then he bides his time before shooting Skeeter."

Weston nodded. "It fits."

"Hey, guys, I'm gonna be the voice of dissent here." Megan leaned her elbows on the table. "Are you sure Chad is sophisticated enough to have pulled this off? He doesn't strike me as a criminal mastermind. For starters, he's openly hostile. If he was trying to hide his actions, screaming at me in front of half a dozen lawmen wasn't a good idea. He's also made threats before and never acted on them. Even his actions last night weren't terribly smart. He didn't even try to disguise himself."

"Could be arrogance," Weston said. "Chad may believe he's untouchable because of his father."

Luke drained the last of his coffee. "He could also be crazy like a fox. By being openly hostile, we think he's incapable of a well-plotted murder. But I think Chad's smarter than most give him credit for."

"Hmm, I hadn't thought about it that way." Megan fiddled with the key hanging from the chain around her neck. "I wish we could figure out what evidence my aunt uncovered. I have the sinking feeling she found Franny's journals and hid them somewhere."

Luke shook his head. "It might not be the journal. The gun used to kill Franny is still missing. June may have uncovered it."

"Whatever it is, she hid it well. We haven't been able to located anything that key goes to," Weston said. He stood and stretched, his fingers brushing the ceiling. "I'd better be on my way, guys. I'm going to interview the friends Skeeter was on the hunting trip with again. Maybe something new will shake loose. Try to keep yourselves out of trouble while I'm gone, okay?"

Luke flashed a grin to his friend. "We'll try."

Megan wagged her eyebrows. "But we make no promises."

"Ha-ha. Ya'll are so funny." He opened the back door. "Keep it up and I'm gonna get the boss to put you on house arrest."

With that parting warning, Weston left. Megan stood. She picked up her mug, along with Weston's, and took them over to the sink. "Let's go to the Wake Up Cafe. Rosa messaged earlier and asked if I would stop by this afternoon."

"I don't think it's a good idea for you to be wandering around town."

She spun to face him. "Thank goodness, because I don't intend on *wandering*. I'm going to see my aunt's friend and continue with the investigation."

His lips flattened and his jaw took on a stubborn edge. He added his own cup to the sink. "Megs—"

"Don't even think about it." She narrowed her gaze. "We made a deal, remember?"

"That was made before a madman shot at you."

"Doesn't change the deal. I'm not going to be scared away from proving my brother's innocence. I came here for a reason and I intend to see it through." She kept her gaze locked on him. "You can't prevent me from doing this, Luke. I make my own choices."

"I know that." He seemed to wrestle with his thoughts before sighing. "I don't want you to get hurt, Megs. You could've died."

The tremble in his voice was slight, but she heard it. Megan placed a hand on his chest, right over his heart. It thumped against her palm.

"Would you stop working as a Texas Ranger? It's dangerous. You could die."

"It's my job. It's..."

"It's worth the risk." She leaned closer, the heat of his body, the feelings buried in the icy blue of his eyes pulling her in. "And this is worth it to me, Luke."

He brushed her mouth with his. The kiss was soft and sweet, and Megan's heart ached for what she'd lost. What she'd thrown away so carelessly. It terrified her to think she might not be able to get it back.

SEVENTEEN

The Wake Up Cafe was at the corner of Main and Second in the center of town. Dark wood floor and plush chairs gave the space a comfortable feel. Megan breathed in the scent of fresh-ground coffee mingled with blue-berry muffins. Several of the tables had patrons and jazz music mingled with murmured voices. A couple of youngsters played in the children's area. Luke fell into step beside her as they crossed the cafe.

"Hey, Gerdie." Megan greeted the young woman behind the counter with a smile. "How are you today?"

"Fine." She shoved her glasses up on her nose and shifted on her feet. Her glossy hair was loose today, tumbling over her narrow shoulders. "What can I get for you?"

They placed their orders and someone called Megan's name. She turned as Kyle approached from the rear. His eyes were watery and his complexion pale. He held out a hand to prevent her from hugging him in greeting.

"I've caught my uncle's cold. I don't want to give it to you." Kyle sniffled, shifting the motorcycle helmet in his left hand to his right. "How are you, Megs?"

"I'm hanging in there."

Gerdie set a to-go cup on the counter with a snap. "Here you go, Kyle. I added lemon and honey to the tea."

"You're an angel." He retrieved his drink, and the chains on his boots jingled. He turned back to Megan and Luke, lowering his voice. "How's the investigation going?"

"We're making progress." Megan frowned. "Kyle, do you remember Chad talking with Wade at Franny's party?"

He stared at the floor in thought. "Ummm, yeah, I do. It was weird because Chad and Wade weren't such good friends, you know. But Wade is one of those guys who's relaxed. He'll talk to anyone."

Megan passed a quick glance to Luke. His theory might be right after all. If Chad was close enough to her brother to steal his phone, then he could've framed him.

Kyle took a sip of his tea. "Come to think of it, Wade talked to many people that night. You know most of the sheriff's department cycled through, and he was friendly with all of them because of his work with your aunt. Lots of Franny's friends are rodeo people because of her brother and dad. It was a crowd."

"Did you notice anyone act strangely that night?" Luke asked.

"Naw." Kyle caught Gerdie's eye and waved her over. "Hey, on the night of Franny's party, did you notice anything weird?"

The young woman blinked at him, clearly caught off guard by the question.

Kyle laughed. "Sorry. That was blunt."

"Gerdie, I didn't know you were at the party that night." Megan racked her brain, trying to determine if there was an interview for her in Franny's file. She didn't remember seeing one, but that didn't mean much, since half of the file was missing. "Did the investigators talk to you?"

Gerdie swallowed hard. "They did, but I couldn't tell them much. I was only there for a short while. And no, sorry, I didn't notice anything strange."

"That's okay. It was worth asking."

"I'd better get moving." Kyle sniffed again. "My bed is calling my name. If you guys need anything, let me know."

"Thanks. We will."

Gerdie went back to filling their order, and Rosa came through the back entrance. She beelined over, her brows furrowed and eyes shadowed with worry.

"Megan, Luke, thanks for stopping by."

"Of course." Megan patted the older woman's arm. "Is everything okay?"

"It's fine." Rosa glanced over her shoulder and leaned closer. "Bessie came over this morning to quilt and we got to talking. We may have news about the case that could help."

167

Megan's heart leaped, but she resisted asking questions. Clearly, her aunt's friend wanted to speak with them about it in private.

Rosa quickly added two more coffees to the order, along with a plate of blueberry muffins. "And Gerdie, could you bring everything over to the house?"

Her niece nodded as she flipped on the bean grinder. "Sure, Aunt Rosa."

"Come on." Rosa waved for Luke and Megan to follow her. "Bessie's working at my place."

She led them to a door in the back. A small courtyard separated the coffee shop from the rest of the property. When she opened the door to her home, a clamor of barking erupted. Two Chihuahuas raced around the corner.

"Fudge and Cookie, stop that right now," Rosa scolded, but in a singsong tone that did nothing to halt the yapping dogs. They circled the guests like attack drones.

"Watch your ankles," Megan whispered to Luke before following Rosa down the hall.

A whirring sound stopped and started and then stopped again. When they entered the kitchen, Bessie was seated, peering at the fabric in her hands over the edge of her reading glasses. A multicolored scarf was wrapped around her head and on the plank table in front of her was a sewing machine, bobbins, and a large quilting hoop.

Bessie looked up and her entire face brightened with

a smile. She started to rise from the chair. "Megan! Luke!"

Megan waved her down, quickly closing the distance to give the other woman a hug. Luke kissed her cheek.

"It's so good to see the both of you. Thanks for coming."

"Of course." Something nipped Megan's ankle, and she shifted to avoid the yapping dog. "Rosa mentioned you might have information about the case we're working on."

"Yes. Sit, sit." Bessie waved to the chairs at the table. "I didn't reach out earlier because I haven't been paying much attention to the town news. I had my chemo a couple of days ago and it knocked the wind right out of me. Today's the first day I'm feeling myself, and I came right over here to visit with Rosa."

Bessie talked a mile a minute and Megan's head was spinning as she pulled out a chair. Luke removed his hat and joined her.

Rosa took a seat next to Bessie. The dogs, thankfully, hopped up next to her. She picked up the quilting hoop and started adding stitches to the cloth. "I told Bessie everything about the investigation this morning while we were sewing."

"I'm working on this quilt for my nephew. He's graduating high school this year, going to A&M in the fall, and this is for his bed at college." Bessie opened up the fabric and frowned. "Shoot. My stitching's crooked. Megan, dear, can you remove these for me?"

"Uhhh, I don't know how—"

"I'll do it." Luke reached for the fabric and some sort of weird tool. "Mrs. Granger, you have us on the edge of our seats. What's going on?"

"Right, well, Rosa mentioned when June had her accident she might've been coming from Woodville. Now, your aunt didn't talk about her cases often, Megan, but there was one she kept asking us to pray about. Quentin Purdue. Young kid, around eighteen or so. He died of a supposed overdose last year, but his grandmother wasn't buying it. She hired June a while back to look into the matter."

"Remember when you asked me about Woodville at church?" Rosa asked. "I knew it rang a bell, but I couldn't remember why. Bessie remembered Quentin's grandmother lives out that way."

Megan frowned. The case wasn't familiar, but June didn't discuss everything with her.

"When did my aunt start working the case?"

Bessie fiddled with the end of her scarf. "I'd say around three months ago. It was something of a rush because the grandmother is very ill. June wanted to get to the bottom of the case before she died."

Gerdie entered the kitchen, her soft-soled shoes squeaking against the linoleum. She set a bag down on the table and the scent of muffins tickled Megan's nose. From the laundry room, the washing machine started banging.

"Gerdie, hon, would you close that door?" Rosa

asked. "Silly washing machine walks all over the room when it starts the spin cycle."

Luke ripped out the last stitch and handed the fabric back to Bessie. She perched her glasses on her nose and studied his work.

"Luke, dear, you did a fantastic job. Oh, your momma raised you right by teaching you how to sew. I wish more men were like you."

Despite the seriousness of the conversation, Megan's mouth twitched, and she nudged Luke under the table with her foot. It hadn't been his mother who taught him. Hank could wield a needle and thread better than any seamstress.

Color rose in Luke's cheeks, and he cleared his throat. "Mrs. Granger, you were telling us about Quentin."

"Right." Bessie nodded. "Like I said, the police are convinced Quentin died of an overdose, but June was also certain he was murdered."

Gerdie stumbled, a plate for the muffins in her hand, and Luke caught her before she could fall. A blush flooded Gerdie's face, and she muttered, "Sorry."

Megan leaned on the table. "Why did June believe he'd been murdered?"

Bessie grabbed a straight pin out of a stuffed tomato. "Well, I don't rightly know. Your aunt didn't give us a play-by-play of her cases, dear. But the Wednesday before her accident, she asked for extra prayers. Made me think maybe she was making progress on Quentin's case, and I was sure to send up a message to the good Lord asking for His help."

Rosa nodded in agreement.

"What about Franny's murder? Did she ever talk about that?"

"Only a bit here and there. Honestly, I thought she'd given up on that investigation a long time ago."

Megan took the coffee Gerdie offered, her mind whirling with the new information. She'd also thought her aunt was done looking into her brother's innocence. Was it possible she'd stumbled across new evidence while working Quentin's case?

"Anyway, even though I wasn't caught up on everything going on, I did mention this to Brent after I heard of June's car accident," Bessie continued. "I thought it might be pertinent. I mean, Megan, I always said your aunt missed her calling as a NASCAR driver. She liked her gas pedal, but she never had an accident. I didn't believe for one moment she went into the ravine on her own."

"When you told Brent about it, what did he say?" Luke asked.

Megan didn't shift positions, but she heard the undertone hidden in Luke's voice. He was furious.

"Oh, he told me not to worry myself about it. You know my boy, Luke. But when Rosa mentioned you thought June was in Woodville...well, I didn't feel right about not saying something to you. Just in case it slipped Brent's mind."

Luke's muscles were rigid, and a headache was brewing in the base of his skull as he stepped into the bullpen of the sheriff's department. It was Friday afternoon, and most of the desks were empty. Dan's office was dark, the door closed, as was the sheriff's.

"Wait here," he told Megan, pointing to a chair at an empty desk. "I'll be right back."

She nodded and sat down. Luke was thankful she didn't put up a fuss. Yes, this concerned her as well, but the conversation with Brent would be easier without an audience. And probably more honest.

He marched through the bullpen to the conference room they'd taken over as a command center for the investigation. Brent was inside, writing notes on the whiteboard.

"Did your mother tell you about a case June was working on?" Luke asked, cutting straight to the chase.

Brent blinked, and his mouth dropped open slightly. "Yeah. She mentioned it a couple of days ago."

"And you didn't think it was important enough to tell me about?" He pointed a finger at the photograph of June's wrecked car hanging in the middle of the whiteboard. "That's my case up there, Brent. Anything that could pertain to it, I should know about."

"That's...it doesn't..." He took a deep breath. "Okay, hold on. I get why you're ticked off, but the two cases aren't connected."

"How can you be so sure?"

"Because Quentin Perdue died of an overdose. I

know June was suspicious, but the guy was an addict and the batch of drugs he'd taken was bad. There was nothing more to it."

"Your mother mentioned June may have found something new on the case?"

Brent fiddled with his wedding ring. "I know, but I visited Camilla Perdue, Quentin's grandmother. She's had several strokes and the last one made it impossible for her to answer any of my questions. The caregiver I spoke to said June hadn't been there on the day of her accident. Honestly, Luke, there's nothing to the case."

It all sounded good, but Luke couldn't let go of the fact that Brent never mentioned it. It made it seem like he had something to hide.

"Who worked the case?"

Brent hesitated. "Dan did."

It could be a coincidence. The sheriff's office didn't have many investigators, but he wasn't taking chances.

"I want to see the file," Luke said.

"Don't do this."

"What?" He crossed his arms over his chest. "My job?"

"Oh, come on, Luke. You may be a ranger and immune to political pressure, but you still have to work with the local law enforcement. Opening another one of Dan's cases without good cause will make it seem like you're gunning for the guy. It's a terrible idea, and it could set you back professionally."

Luke's gaze narrowed. "This is the second time you've tried to warn me about this case."

"Because it's personal for you, and there's a reason why we don't work cases that are personal. The decisions you make aren't always logical when emotions are involved. I'm also your friend and I'm looking out for you."

"Is that it? Or is there something more? After all, if Dan is elected, he'll become your boss."

"That's incredibly insulting." Brent stiffened and color rose in his cheeks. "Is that what you think of me?"

Luke didn't know what to think. Every time he turned around, someone else was hiding something about this case. Then again, maybe he was being a touch paranoid. Brent had never given him a reason to distrust him.

"I'm sorry," Luke said. "It's been a frustrating couple of days."

"I get it." He took a deep breath and ran a hand over his bald head. "Luke, listen, we all want the same thing. I know Dan can get intense, but there's no indication he's done anything wrong."

He valued Brent's opinion, but Luke had lost a lot of faith in Dan after finding him in the evidence room threatening Megan. No lawman—even an angry one—should act like that.

"Tread lightly," Brent continued. "You don't want to get a reputation as a cop who attacks other cops. That won't endear you to the local law enforcement. Don't let your feelings about this case cloud your judgment and ruin the career you've worked so hard to build."

Luke was sorely tempted to throw Brent's last piece of advice right back at him. They both had personal involvements and ties. The chances of Dan becoming the next sheriff were high, and everyone in the building would be cautious about being seen as disloyal.

It made him wonder if there was anyone in the sheriff's department he could trust.

EIGHTEEN

Camilla Perdue lived in a two-story farmhouse on the outskirts of Woodville. Weeds poked out of the flowerbeds, and the siding was in desperate need of a new coat of paint. A large dog on the far side of the yard jumped and barked furiously when they got out of the vehicle.

Megan eyed the beast with trepidation. "Do you think the chain will hold him?"

Luke prayed it would. He'd already put himself between her and the dog as they went up the walk, but he couldn't resist teasing her.

"I thought you liked dogs."

"I do, but that doesn't mean I want to be lunch."

He chuckled and pressed on the doorbell. Nothing happened. Opening the screen door, he gave the inner one a solid rap with his knuckles. Moments later, it was opened by a freckle-faced redhead around three or four wearing a cartoon T-shirt.

"Hi," he greeted her. "Is your mommy home?"

She narrowed her gaze and put her tiny hands on her hips. "Are you a bad guy or a good guy?"

Beside him, Megan pressed her lips together as if she was holding in a laugh. Luke opened his jacket to reveal the ranger badge pinned to his shirt.

"I'm a police officer. That makes me a good guy."

"Vivian!" A woman hurried down the stairs. She was barefoot, wearing sweatpants and a stained shirt. A white cloth was slung over one shoulder and she was carrying an infant. "Haven't I told you not to open the door to strangers?"

"But, Momma, he's a policeman."

The girl's mother looked up, seeming to register their identities for the first time. Her eyes, shadowed with dark circles, widened slightly.

"Sorry to disturb you, ma'am." Luke flashed his badge again. "Texas Ranger Luke Tatum and this is Megan Hunt. Is this Camilla Perdue's residence?"

"It is. I'm her granddaughter, Ruby." She waved them inside, her gaze never leaving Megan's face. "You look so familiar…"

"My aunt is June Carpenter—"

"Oh, my goodness, yes." Ruby's hand fluttered to her forehead, and she swiped her bangs out of her eyes. "I used to be a makeup artist, so faces are a big thing for me. You have June's mouth and chin. How is your aunt? She hasn't been by this week and…"

Her gaze skipped to Luke, the joy fleeing from her expression. "Is everything okay?"

Luke glanced at Vivian, still watching them with an eagle-eyed gaze. Ruby caught on right away and said, "Vivian, honey, you can go into the living room and watch TV with Granny until dinner is ready."

The little girl flew off, her long hair fluttering behind her, and disappeared around a corner. Megan gently explained about June's accident.

Ruby hugged her infant closer. "That's horrible. I knew something wasn't right when she didn't come by."

"How do you know June?" Luke asked.

"My grandmother hired her to look into my cousin's death a few months ago. Granny was convinced Quentin didn't die of an overdose."

"Would it be possible for me to speak with Mrs. Perdue?" Luke asked.

"I'm afraid not." She sighed. "Come with me."

She led them to the entrance of the living room. An elderly woman with thin white hair and bloodshot eyes slouched in a wheelchair. On the television, a game show played. Vivian bounced on the couch and the elderly woman's eyes followed the child. Her lips twisted into a grimace.

"That's Granny. She's smiling, but the strokes have made it harder for her mobility." Ruby lowered her voice. "I'm afraid she doesn't remember much either. She was doing okay until the stroke last month. As you can see, questioning her won't be possible."

Luke swallowed back his frustration. "A deputy from the Medina County Sheriff's Office stopped by last week. Did he speak to you?"

"No, but there's a neighbor who comes twice a week for a few hours. Just to give me a chance to run errands. My husband is deployed overseas, so I don't have any help."

The baby in her arms started crying, stretching chubby arms out in anger. Ruby bounced the infant and half waved for them to follow her.

"Come into the kitchen. I have to get dinner ready. I didn't live here with my cousin and Granny at the time of his death, but I can try to answer your questions."

The kitchen was spacious but in desperate need of renovation. Ruby tried to set the baby down in a swing, but the infant only screamed louder.

Ruby sighed. "How does she always know when I'm about to cook?"

"May I?" Megan asked, stepping forward. "I'm sure a moment's peace and two free hands isn't something you get often."

"Would you? Thank you so much. I'm trying to keep Vivian on a consistent schedule, but it's not easy between taking care of the baby and Granny."

"I bet not."

Megan scooped the infant into her arms and murmured sweet words. Luke's gaze lingered on them. For half a second, he let himself imagine it was their child she was holding. The idea should have terrified him, but the memory of their kiss from earlier in the day melded with the image and his heart galloped.

"I suppose you've done a background check on Quentin and saw he was arrested in the past for drugs,"

Ruby said, pulling a package of ground beef out of the refrigerator. "That's a big part of the reason why the investigators were convinced he'd overdosed."

Her words brought reality crashing down on Luke, along with every reason why a relationship with Megan wouldn't work. He'd had a hand in putting her brother in prison. Whatever feelings lingered between them could only be temporary. There was no way to survive the hurt long-term.

Luke shifted his focus back to where it belonged: on the case.

"Why was your grandmother convinced otherwise?" he asked.

"Because Quentin was clean and regularly attending NA meetings." Her lips flattened into a thin line. "He was also scared. Granny told me he'd gotten messed up with some nasty people. She begged him to go to the police, but he refused."

"Do you know why?"

"Anything I tell you would be a guess, but my impression was Quentin was scared of the cops." She gripped the frying pan handle and stirred the meat as it cooked. "I'm not sure if that's because he did something illegal he didn't want them to know about or if it was for a different reason."

Luke weighed the information. If Quentin had been involved in selling drugs, it would make sense he'd be nervous about going to the police.

"What did June uncover?" he asked.

Ruby opened a cabinet and pulled down a can of

tomato sauce. "I don't know a lot. She and Granny insisted on keeping the investigation very quiet. June told me the less I knew, the better."

Luke stiffened, and his gaze shot to the baby before settling back on Ruby. What had June uncovered that made her so scared? Who was Quentin working with?

Megan rocked the baby. "Did my aunt come by here last Friday?"

Ruby nodded. "In the afternoon. I'd say around two thirty or so, but she didn't stay long. She chatted a couple of minutes with Granny and left."

It took about twenty minutes to drive from Cardin to the Perdues' ranch. If June only stayed a few minutes, that still left an hour and a half of her time unaccounted for. So where else did she go?

Ruby paused in her stirring. "Wait, there was something else. June went in Quentin's room before she left."

Luke leaned forward. "Quentin's room is still intact?"

"Oh yeah." She pointed to an area off the kitchen with her ladle. "It's over there. Granny insisted we keep it as-is."

"Mind if we look around?"

"No, go ahead." She took the baby from Megan. "Thanks for holding her."

The bedroom wasn't large. A twin bed sat underneath a window covered in plaid curtains. The closet was cocked open, neatly hung shirts visible, shoes lined up in a row on the floor. Photos of Quentin lined the bureau. His shaggy hair hung in his eyes, and he favored jeans and a western-style shirt.

"He's won awards for calf roping." Megan pointed out the belt buckles intermingled with the pictures. "Wonder if he ran in the same rodeo circles with Chad?"

"It's a possibility."

On the wall, hung as if they were decorations, were various guns. An inscription on the cylinder of a revolver caught Luke's eye. He frowned.

Megan stepped closer, the scent of honeysuckle following. "What is it?"

"That gun..." He pointed to it. "I've seen it before. It was confiscated from a parolee along with a bunch of others."

"Are you sure?"

"Positive." His chest was tight. It hurt to breathe. "That inscription is unique, and the original owner is deceased without any living relatives."

She frowned. "But...if it was confiscated...and not returned to the original owner, that means—"

"It should be in the Medina County Sheriff Department's evidence room. So how did Quentin get his hands on it?"

***

Megan lifted her cell phone, angling it to eliminate the glare from the lamp on the nightstand. She stifled a yawn. It'd been a long day.

"After we found the gun in Quentin's room, Luke called his superior," she said. "They'll audit the evidence room at the sheriff's department to see if things are being stolen."

On screen, Grace tucked a braid behind her ear. "Doesn't the sheriff's evidence room have cameras?"

Megan leaned against the headboard. "Nope. It's a small department with minimal resources and, like many rural areas, a big drug problem. A deputy will do a bust and bring in the contraband. A small portion of it gets sent to the state lab for testing to determine the type of substance it is—cocaine, meth, etc—but the rest stays in the evidence room. Eventually, the drugs or the guns are supposed to be destroyed after the case is brought to trial. But someone could steal some or all of the contraband and then claim it's been destroyed when actually it's being resold."

"And you think Quentin was working with someone in the sheriff's department?"

"Yep. It adds a layer of protection if you have someone acting a go-between. Say a deputy wants to steal cocaine and sell it. He doesn't want to run the risk the buyers will recognize him as a law enforcement officer. So he arranges for someone else to be the seller, in this case Quentin."

Her friend nodded. "That makes sense."

"We were focusing on the wrong motive." Megan blew out a breath. "Franny worked in the evidence room, and I suspect, she uncovered the thefts and was killed because of it."

Grace rested her head on her hand. "If that's true,

why didn't Franny tell Sheriff Franklin what was going on?"

"That's a good question. He claims he had no idea, but he could be lying. Sheriff Franklin was at Franny's party on the night of her murder. He only stayed ten minutes or so, but that's all the time it would've taken to steal Wade's cell phone and hide it in the couch cushions."

"So, it could be anyone in the department. How much money are we talking about, do you think?"

"A lot. Luke told me last month the sheriff's deputies confiscated a shipment of cocaine on its way north. The street value exceeded fifty thousand dollars."

Her eyes widened. "Wow."

"My sentiments exactly."

Grace drummed her nails on the desk. "And what about Skeeter?"

"My guess is that Franny told him about the thefts and the killer got wind of it." Megan rolled her head to stretch out the tight muscles in her neck. "I don't know if Skeeter ever talked to June because her notes were destroyed in the fire."

"Do you still want me to run the Dickersons' financials?"

"Yes. Quentin participated in calf-roping and Chad was a bull rider. Maybe there's a link there. I don't want to rule out a thread of investigation yet, even if it's going onto the back burner."

Their forensic accountant was expensive and could work a lot quicker than the Texas Rangers. He didn't need warrants or probable cause to dig, and he had plenty of connections to countries where off-shore accounts were common.

"How's June doing?" Grace asked.

"Same. I just came from visiting her a little while ago. She's strong and the doctors are still hopeful but cautious." Megan ran her finger over the edge of the Bible on her nightstand. "Your present came today. Thank you."

Her friend smiled. "Keep searching for the truth, Megs, but also keep up with those prayers. He's listening."

They talked for a few more minutes, and after Megan hung up, she reached for the Bible. It had a delicate woven string attached as a bookmark. Opening to the page, she smiled. Grace had flagged Ecclesiastes 3:17, and Megan read it out loud.

"God will bring into judgment both the righteous and the wicked, for there will be a time for every activity, a time to judge every deed."

She closed her eyes and bowed her head.

Lord, I don't know why things have to be this way. Why did Wade have to go to prison for a crime he didn't commit? Why did June have to be injured? Why did Franny have to die? It hurts, God. It makes me angry. But I still surrender to Your will. I know things must happen in their own time. I'll keep looking for the truth, so I hope You will use me as Your instrument, but I won't fight You anymore. I'll have faith.

A peace enveloped her, settling in her spirit like a

warm, comforting blanket. For the first time, Megan sensed things would be okay. She set the Bible back down on the nightstand and went to search for Luke.

He was in the living room. The fireplace was lit, providing warmth. Her slippers didn't make a sound against the rug in the hall and she paused in the doorway, taking in the scene. Luke sat on the couch, his brow furrowed in thought, writing on a pad of paper. Bristles shadowed his strong jaw, and the firelight played with the edges of his chiseled features. Jax was sprawled at his feet, long ears flopped on the rug, and Archimedes was tucked up against his side.

"You all look very cozy together," she remarked. "Did your parents go to bed?"

"Yep. You just missed them, but Mom left you some hot chocolate."

He jerked his chin to the mug on the table. Mini-marshmallows floated on top of the dark liquid.

"It's a new recipe. She wants a report tomorrow morning on whether this one is better than yesterday's. Hank and I both gave our opinion, but Mom wasn't interested."

"Hank gave his in grunts, and yours was probably 'good' with a shoulder shrug."

His mouth quirked. "How did you know?"

They laughed, and Megan scooped up the still-warm hot chocolate before settling in on the couch. Jax opened one eye, and she patted him in greeting. He sighed and went back to sleep.

"What are you working on?" she asked, sipping her

drink. It was rich and smooth, and the sweet chocolate mingled with the faint scent of cinnamon. Definitely better than yesterday's.

"I'm making notes about the case using the potential new angle." He passed the notepad over to her. "If someone is stealing from the evidence room, we need to move fast. The thief has had a lot of time to clean up his tracks. Based on everything else, the perpetrator is organized and methodical. I don't expect this to be any different."

She nodded and scanned the paper. He'd made notations next to his top suspects. Dan and Sheriff Franklin were high on the list, but so was an unexpected addition.

Her mouth dropped open. "You suspect Brent might be involved?"

"He's financially struggling because of his mom's cancer. He has access to the evidence room, and we left him alone with the saddles, which gave him plenty of time to add the trackers."

With a sinking feeling in the pit of her stomach, Megan realized he was right.

"I also can't overlook that he was an investigator on Franny's case," Luke continued. "It would've been easy for him to manipulate or hide evidence. He's also warned me about rocking the boat and upsetting Dan."

"He did? When?"

"When you first arrived in town and then again today when I confronted him about Quentin's case. Brent claims it's because he's looking out for me, but with these new developments, I wonder if he's hiding something."

"I suppose the financial trouble applies to Cindy as well. She's also very organized and methodical." She bit her lip. "Could it be possible two people are working together? Like Brent and Cindy? Or Cindy and the sheriff?"

"I won't take anything off the table. I'm hoping the audit of the evidence room will give us a better impression of how much is being stolen. The more that's missing, the more likely it is that many people are involved. There have been cases of entire departments taking a cut."

Megan took another sip of her hot chocolate, letting the warm liquid soothe her nerves. She didn't want to imagine the entire Medina County Sheriff's Department being corrupt. It was too much. She scanned his paper again.

"I don't know, Luke. Like we said earlier, this perpetrator is methodical. I could buy two people working together, but not a whole crowd. The more people who know, the greater the potential for exposure. It defeats the purpose of having Quentin as your go-between."

"Good point." Luke leaned his head back and stared at the ceiling. "I hate this."

He didn't need to explain. There was a brotherhood among those that carried the badge and a fierce loyalty that went with it.

"I know."

"I'm sorry." He rubbed his face. "Your brother's in prison and I'm bemoaning about rooting out a crooked cop."

189

"Don't apologize. These people are your friends and our neighbors. There's nothing wrong with wanting to believe in their goodness."

His gaze locked on hers. Midnight blue in the firelight, nearly black, Luke's eyes entranced her. He brushed a lock of hair out of her face and tucked it behind her ear, leaving a trail of molten heat in its wake.

Her breath hitched and her chest felt tight. Luke's fingers scraped across the sensitive skin of her ear, briefly touching the gold hoop earring before reaching out and taking the mug from her hand. He set it on the table and pulled her into his arms.

His lips brushed against hers. The faint taste of hot chocolate lingered on his lips, and Megan's heart rate skyrocketed. The kisses were tender and sweet. When he pulled back, she traced the faint scar at the corner of his mouth. His hero mark. The one he'd earned defending a woman from her abusive husband in the hall outside a courtroom years ago. The one that reminded her of the day he stole her heart.

He still had it. Her heart. Her love. The truth hit her like a sledgehammer to the head and was as undeniable as the air she breathed.

"Luke, I love you." The words tumbled out before she could think about them or even second-guess the decision to say them out loud. "I don't think I ever stopped loving you."

He let out a breath. "Megs—"

His phone rang, cutting off whatever Luke was about to say. He simultaneously grabbed it from the coffee table and stood from the couch. It was a physical distance that mirrored the emotional one. He'd only said her name, but she had years of experience in reading Luke. There'd been hesitation riding the timbre of his voice.

He cared about her, that much she knew. Maybe he even loved her. But that didn't translate into forever. And Luke would never make promises or say words he didn't intend to keep.

"Ranger Tatum." He put the phone to his ear. "Never mind, Lieutenant, I was awake."

Megan sat up straighter. Luke's boss wouldn't call this late unless she had news. He listened intently, his posture growing rigid. A muscle in his jaw worked.

"Ten tomorrow morning. Yes, ma'am, I'll be there." Luke's gaze shot to her. "May I make one request? Can Megan sit in on the meeting?"

He paused. "Thank you, ma'am. We'll see you then."

Luke hung up and shoved his phone in his pocket. "The gun recovered from Quentin's bedroom is a match to the one reported stolen by the original owner."

"So it's official. Someone stole it from the evidence room."

He nodded. "There's more, Megs. They did a ballistic analysis of the weapon and came up with a match. It was the gun used to kill Franny."

NINETEEN

Nervous energy pulsed through Luke's veins the next morning as he paced the conference room in the state police department. He'd arrived early for the meeting, along with Megan, and explained the latest developments in the case to his fellow rangers. Now, they were waiting for Lieutenant Rodriguez to arrive.

"I don't see anything but a blob." Weston tilted Grady's phone one way and then the other. On screen, an ultrasound image turned and resized. "A nice blob, but still...just a blob."

"Thank goodness you became a ranger and not a doctor." Grady snatched his phone and turned it long ways. He pointed at the screen. "Right there. That's the head. See the eyes and the mouth?"

He squinted. "Uhhh, sure."

Grady let out an exasperated sound. "Luke, help me out here."

He'd already had his viewing session and agreed with

192

Weston. He held up his hands. "There's a reason I'm not a doctor either."

"Show me." Megan scooted closer and took the phone. She smiled. "I see it. It's obvious. His head is here. There's the nose and his eyes. Is that his hand near his mouth?"

"Yes." Grady beamed. "He's sucking his thumb. Doesn't he look like me?"

"Ugh." Weston shuddered and winced. "Let's hope not. Of the two of you, Tara is the better looking one. By far. You better hope all your kids come out looking like her."

They all laughed.

Lieutenant Rodriguez strolled in, and the entire room snapped to attention. Luke took his seat next to Megan. His boss set a notepad and pen down on the table before pulling out a chair.

"You're caught up to date on the recent developments in the case?" she asked.

Heads nodded around the table.

"Good, because I've got another one. The revolver we recovered yesterday wasn't the only thing stolen from the evidence room. Various contraband, including weapons and controlled substances, are missing."

The news wasn't shocking, but it still felt like a sharp blade in Luke's gut. Members of the badge were supposed to protect and serve. Those that betrayed the mission didn't deserve his loyalty or understanding.

From the tense looks on his colleagues' faces, they were having the same thoughts.

"How long has it been going on?" Luke asked.

"Several years." Her lips thinned. "And it's extensive. I had investigators working overnight to prevent the staff and deputies from figuring out what we were looking into. Sheriff Franklin was the only one aware of the new direction our investigation has taken, and he's agreed to cooperate in any way possible."

"How much do we trust the sheriff?" Grady asked.

"I've had a background done on him overnight as well. It's preliminary, of course, but there are no red flags. Sheriff Franklin even consented to a search of his home and provided information on his bank accounts. It doesn't rule him out completely, but it makes me a lot more confident that he's not involved."

Beside him, Megan let out a sigh. Luke echoed the sentiment. He liked Sheriff Franklin, and he hated to think the corruption went all the way to the top.

"Other than the Smith & Wesson, no other contraband was found in Quentin's room." Lieutenant Rodriguez nodded in his direction. "Good eyes, Luke."

"The inscription on the outside of the weapon made it unique, thank goodness. Otherwise I might not have caught it."

Weston frowned. "Which begs the question. Why would Quentin—if he's the killer—use that particular weapon to murder Franny? It's easy to identify as being stolen. And why keep it?"

"Maybe he didn't realize the gun was unique until later," Grady suggested. "If that part of the cylinder is under the frame, the inscription isn't visible. Or could be he simply kept it as a trophy."

Weston nodded. "A memory of the kill. Yeah. That works."

"There is another possibility," Luke said. "According to his family, Quentin wanted out of his troubled lifestyle. He started going to Narcotics Anonymous and so forth. Maybe the gun was leverage against the person he was working for. I talked to forensics this morning. There were traces of fingerprint powder on the weapon and it's not the type used by the state lab."

Megan sucked in a breath. "My aunt dusted it."

"That's my guess."

"If that's true, then someone had to tell her where to look." Lieutenant Rodriguez made a notation on her pad. "Grady, you take the lead on that. I want every single one of Quentin's friends and associates interviewed. Somebody knows something."

"Yes, ma'am."

She turned her steel-eyed gaze to Megan. "Did your brother know Quentin?"

"No. I spoke with my brother's attorney this morning. Grace confirmed Wade didn't know him."

"Do we know if Quentin was at Franny's party that night?" Weston asked. "Is there any link between him and Franny other than the murder weapon?"

"It's possible they knew each other. Quentin competed in rodeos and Franny's brother, Chad, is a former bull rider." Megan frowned. "We should talk to Kyle Franklin. He was a competitive calf roper as well.

Maybe he can tell us if he saw Quentin at Franny's party."

"Franklin?" Lieutenant Rodriguez cocked her head. "Is he related to the sheriff?"

"It's his nephew. Kyle's been helpful in giving us information. I think he'll be willing to share anything he knows."

Luke nodded his agreement, and his boss made another note.

"Good. The two of you can do that this afternoon. Weston, you and I will tackle the Medina County Sheriff's Department. We need to start at the top with Chief Deputy Dan Carter and work our way down. Alibis, financials, the whole works." She tapped her pen against the pad. "Right now, I'm going to treat these cases like one. Quentin is the link. Either he killed Franny, or he was working for the person who did."

Lieutenant Rodriguez squared her shoulders. "We don't stop until we find every single person involved."

The drive back to Cardin was mostly made in silence. Menacing clouds, thick with rain, greeted them when Luke exited the freeway and took the turn toward Kyle's property. An occasional lightning bolt lit up the sky. Luke needed to keep his mind on the case, but last night's conversation with Megan kept creeping in.

He glanced at her out of the corner of his eye. She was deep in thought, evident from the cute wrinkles above the bridge of her nose. Her hair was pulled back in a high ponytail, gracing him with the sweet curve of her cheek and the long column of her neck. Megan rummaged around inside a bag of jelly beans, popped a few in her mouth, and chewed slowly.

He loved her. There wasn't a doubt in his mind about that, but like the brewing thunderstorm in the distance, harsh realities loomed in their future. What happened if he couldn't prove Wade's innocence and get him out of prison? Would Megan leave again? Would the love they have survive a second time?

Luke didn't know, and it terrified him. He'd spent half the night staring at her old engagement ring. The warmth of being in her arms, hearing her say I love you, was overshadowed by the case and his past mistakes.

When he pulled into Kyle's driveway, Megan whistled. "Wow, he's made a lot of improvements to this place. The garage is new, and so is the siding on the house."

"Yeah. He's done most of the work in the last year or so."

Luke rang the bell. It took a long time for Kyle to come to the door. When he finally did, his hair was disheveled and a day's worth of bristles darkened his jaw. He was wearing a worn T-shirt and ripped jeans.

"Sorry." Megan smiled. "Did we wake you?"

"No, I was watching a movie. This cold is brutal." He leaned against the door. "What's up?"

"We need to ask you some questions about Franny's party. Can we come in?"

Kyle hesitated, glancing back into the recesses of the

house. A bolt of lightning lit up the sky followed by a low rumble of thunder and wind scattered pine needles through the yard.

He opened the door with a sigh. "The house is messy at the moment but okay. Come in."

Luke crossed over the threshold and caught a whiff of marijuana smoke. A knot formed in his stomach. He followed Megan into the living room. Empty chip bags littered the coffee table, along with several glasses. One of them held an amber-colored liquid.

Luke craned his neck toward the back bedrooms. "Is anyone else in the house with you?"

"Nope. I just don't do dishes often." Kyle grabbed a couple of glasses and laughed. "Don't go in the laundry room. You'll never make it out alive."

Luke chuckled. "I'm not a fan of laundry myself. Still, do you mind if I look around?"

Kyle frowned and his gaze narrowed. The request made it sound as if he was a suspect, and it clearly put him on edge, but Luke wouldn't ignore his gut instinct.

Megan rolled her eyes. "Good grief, all law enforcement officers are the same. Sheriff Franklin used to do the same thing when he visited June."

Luke's expression never changed as the lie tumbled from her lips. Working with Megan for the last week reminded him of how in tune they were. He hadn't been joking when he told her they made great partners.

Kyle's posture relaxed. "Yeah. Come to think of it, I've done a couple of ride-alongs with my uncle and he did it then too." He set the glasses down on the coffee table. "I'll go with you."

He escorted Luke down the hall. The bedroom doors were open. One had been converted to an office. Most of them were neat, except for the master. The bed was unmade and a pile of dirty glasses sat on the nightstand. The television on the dresser was on, a car chase playing out on the screen.

"Thanks, man," Luke said. He hadn't looked in the closets or under the beds, but asking would've been pushing it. "Appreciate it."

"No problem."

They went back into the living room. Megan had straightened the cushions on the couch and gathered the trash into a pile.

"You don't have to clean up," Kyle said, rubbing the back of his neck. "Gosh, this is embarrassing."

"I don't know why." Megan laughed lightly. "Your nickname in middle school was Pigpen. It's not like you didn't come over to our house and make a disaster there every single weekend."

"And you used to yell at me about it." He picked up a dirty plate. "I miss those days. Things were so simple back then, but we didn't know it."

Luke helped them carry a couple of glasses into the kitchen. Rain pattered against the window. The kitchen wasn't much cleaner than the living room. A half-eaten sandwich and more dirty dishes littered the stained countertop. The tension in Kyle's shoulders went away. Interesting. He didn't like it when they were in the living room.

"What questions do you have for me?" Kyle asked.

"Do you know a Quentin Perdue?" Megan asked, flipping on the faucet and squeezing dish soap into the sink.

"Yeah. I met him back when I used to do cattle-roping competitions at the rodeo. But he died last year from an overdose."

Luke kept his distance, letting Megan take the lead on questioning. She had a relationship with Kyle that went back to childhood and he was more relaxed speaking with her.

"Was Quentin at Franny's birthday party?" She turned off the water. Suds floated in the sink, intermixed with the dirty dishes.

Kyle frowned and leaned against the counter, crossing his arms. He stared at the tile floor for a moment. "Yeah, he was. Why?"

"We received a tip about him."

Megan went back into the living room. Luke followed. Kyle bolted after them. His gaze darted toward the hall before settling back on Megan. She picked up another couch cushion and shook it out.

"Really, Megs—"

"Did Franny know Quentin?" She put the pillow back into position. "Were they friends?"

"I don't think they were close, but yeah, they were friendly. I mean she invited him to her party. But they didn't hang out often. After Franny stopped going to the rodeo with Chad and Skeeter, a lot of the friends she made there drifted off."

Luke meandered over to a bookshelf pretending to examine a baseball trophy. The hallway was clear. Nothing seemed out of place, but Kyle's spine stiffened.

"What about Wade?" Megan asked. "Did he know Quentin?"

"I don't think so." Kyle sniffed. "Wade and Franny didn't become friends until after her rodeo days were over. What's this all about? What kind of tip did you receive about Quentin?"

"We've learned he might be involved in Franny's murder."

Kyle's eyes darted back and forth. "Quentin? That's... that would be weird. I mean, the guy wasn't a saint. I know he was using drugs way back in the rodeo days, but he never struck me as violent. And he was always nice to Franny."

Luke moved back toward the couch and Kyle let out a breath. Something about the bookcase was making him nervous. Megan seemed to notice too because she grabbed an empty bag of chips and crumpled it before reaching for another. Smart woman read his mind. They needed to get Kyle out of the living room so Luke could poke around.

"That's good to know," Megan said. "Did you stay friends with Quentin until his death?"

"No. Come to think of it, Franny's party was the last time I saw him." Kyle frowned. "Seriously, Megs, you don't have to clean."

"You know me. I hate clutter." She handed him another plate. "Here. If we both do it, we'll have the place spic-and-span in no time. Remember the time you and Wade played water balloons inside?"

Kyle chuckled. "June was furious. So were you."

"We made you clean the entire living room from top to bottom."

Megan strolled into the kitchen and Kyle followed. Half listening to their conversation, Luke crossed the living room. He scanned the bookshelves. There wasn't anything out of the ordinary. Belt buckles that served as trophies for cattle roping, knickknacks, and a few crime novels.

A closet was nearby. It was deep enough to be a walk-in and, with the light off, impossible to see inside. Glancing over his shoulder, Luke confirmed Megan and Kyle were still deep in conversation.

He nudged the door inward with his foot and stepped inside, flipping on the light. He sucked in a breath and his mind took quick mental photos. Marijuana, pills, and white powder intermingled with rifles and handguns. Dangling from a pistol was an evidence tag.

A muzzle pressed into the back of his head. Luke froze.

"I knew you were going to be trouble."

TWENTY

The tape binding Megan's wrists was cutting off her circulation. She took a deep breath to calm her racing heart. The couch underneath her sagged and the scent of marijuana made her head hurt. *Lord, we could use some help.*

Beside her, Luke sat stone-faced, his hands cuffed behind his back. His primary weapon along with his backup and his knife sat on the wet bar. Close enough to see but impossible to reach. His gaze was fixed on the two men in front of them, and she knew he was waiting for an opening. But how much could he do with no weapon and his hands behind his back?

"Oh no, oh no. This is bad."

Kyle paced up and down the living room. His steps were frantic, increasing with the pitch of his voice. The hand holding his gun shook.

"This is really bad," he continued. "What are we going to do?"

"What do you think, you idiot," Dan snapped.

The chief deputy took a drag of his cigarette and held the smoke in for a moment before blowing it out.

"We're going to kill them."

Megan swallowed hard. She'd suspected that was the plan, but hearing him say the words in such a cold manner sent fresh terror racing through her. A drop of sweat trickled down her back. Her gaze snapped to the weapon in Dan's hand.

Kyle reared back. "We...we can't do that. That's crazy."

"No, that's self-preservation. There's at least twenty thousand dollars worth of drugs in that closet. Do you know what the prison sentence for that is?"

"I didn't sign up for murder."

Dan shrugged. "You knew the risks."

The horror on Kyle's face wasn't an act. Megan racked her brain, recalling their conversations and everything she knew about the case. Kyle had been the one who confirmed Franny wasn't alone on the night of her murder. He told them about the phone call he'd received. Why would he do that if he was part of it?

He wouldn't. Quentin died a year ago, but Lieutenant Rodriguez said the thefts from the evidence room were going on for a while and were extensive. Dan had to be the one behind it. After Quentin died, he needed a new go-between, and Kyle was it.

"The only question is how we do it," Dan continued, taking another drag on his cigarette before snuffing it out in the ashtray on the coffee table. "The easiest would be to kill them right now and be done with it."

"But it wouldn't be smart." Luke arched his brows, his tone casual, as if he was discussing the weather and not murder. "Do you know how hard it is to dispose of a body? Not to mention the trace evidence that's left behind? I've already informed dispatch I'm here. This is the first place they'll look."

Kyle's breathing sped up. "He's right."

As if on cue, Luke's phone on the wet bar started ringing.

Dan glanced at it and frowned. "Why is Weston calling you?"

"Because he needs to talk to me. If I don't answer, he'll call again," Luke said. "Turn off the phone and he'll know something is wrong."

Kyle swallowed hard. "We can't do this. It'll never work. We'll get caught."

"Don't be stupid." Dan tapped a finger to his temple. "He's screwing with your head. Don't you understand he'll say anything to prevent us from killing him? That doesn't make it true."

Luke's phone rang again. He lifted his chin. "Everything I'm telling you is true, Kyle."

"Shut up," Dan snapped. He grabbed the roll of duct tape and peeled off a piece, shoving it over Luke's mouth. "Shoulda done that in the first place."

Dan grabbed Luke's face, squeezing hard enough to form indentions in the skin, and pushed it back. He put the muzzle of his gun to Luke's throat.

"I'm gonna enjoy shooting you."

Luke glared at him. Despite the weakness of his position, fear didn't flicker across his features. Megan heart flipped, however, and her blood turned to ice.

"Like you did Franny?"

Her voice trembled, but the question worked as she'd hoped to distract Dan. He turned toward her and smirked. Madness glimmered in his eyes.

"What's she talking about?" Kyle's gaze jumped from Dan to Megan and back again. "Did you kill Franny and frame Wade?"

"It was before your time, and it's not your concern. The less you know, the better." Dan released Luke and stepped back. "We'll drive them out to the woods and shoot them there."

Luke's expression never changed, but his posture relaxed a fraction. Megan understood why. The decision to kill them later bought them time, and every minute counted.

He glanced at her and then down before focusing back on the men. She followed his gaze, but there was nothing there. Just the edge of his jacket and pants and...

She inhaled sharply. Luke's car keys were covered by his sports jacket, but they hung from a hook on his belt. If he kept the same habits he had while they were dating, the key to his cuffs should be on that same ring.

"Do you have any tarps?" Dan asked.

Kyle swallowed hard. "In a cabinet above the garage."

"Good. I'll spread them out in the back of your truck." He jerked a thumb over his shoulder to the closet.

"We'll take a gun from there. If we're lucky, the weapon will have been used in a previous crime and it'll be in the system. That'll confuse the investigators."

"I'll get one."

"Wait for me. I don't want them left alone in case either of them tries something." Dan held Kyle's gaze. "I'll be right back. If they so much as blink, shoot them."

He lumbered out of the house. Megan took the opportunity to shift her body on the couch. Her hands were bound behind her back. Finding and unhooking Luke's keys wouldn't be easy, but it was the only chance they had.

Lord, guide my fingers. Help me stay strong.

"You don't have to do this, Kyle." She kept her tone calm and reasonable. "This isn't you."

"How can I avoid it?" He paced the length of the room. "Luke shouldn't have snooped. If he hadn't gone in the closet, then none of this would be happening."

"But it is happening and you have choices. No one is dead yet."

Megan shifted again, as if she was uncomfortable, estimating the key ring's position on Luke's belt. Her fingers slipped under his jacket but found only the soft fabric of his pants.

"You realize Dan is going to pin our murders on you, right?"

Kyle swallowed hard and the hand holding his gun trembled. "No, he won't."

Luke slid down on the couch. Her fingers brushed

against his leather belt and she traced it. From the wet bar, his cell phone started ringing again.

Please, Lord. I hope Weston realizes something is terribly wrong.

"Franny found out that someone was stealing from the evidence room, Kyle. Dan killed her for it and framed Wade." Her mouth was dry, and she licked her lips. "Think about it for a minute. Did you see Dan talking to Wade at Franny's party?"

Kyle's jaw tightened.

Bingo.

Quentin hadn't stolen her brother's phone. Dan had. He'd set up the entire murder and then given Quentin the gun to sell afterward. But things didn't go as planned. Quentin kept the gun and tried to use it as leverage when he decided to change his life. Dan killed him instead, setting up the murder to look like an overdose. Everyone had bought it—except June and Quentin's grandmother.

Luke slouched lower, and the keys touched her palm. She closed her hand around them, her heart pounding.

"Whose truck is Dan spreading the tarps in right now? Not his own. He's using yours. Think about it, Kyle. He's going to turn on you."

"I..." Kyle's gaze darted to Luke's phone. He let out a breath. "He can't. I know too much."

"Quentin probably thought so too."

Kyle's eyes widened and his mouth dropped open. He shook his head and backed up a few paces as if to separate himself from her words. His gaze darted to the windows overlooked the driveway. The unattached garage was just beyond the glass.

There was no sign of Dan, but they needed to hurry. Luke shifted once more, and the keys slid off his belt.

Thank you, Lord.

"The stuff in the closet is bad," she continued. "But it's only drugs and weapons. A good defense attorney might be able to get the evidence thrown out on a technicality. Killing a law enforcement officer in Texas, however, is a capital crime."

Luke's phone rang again.

"Or you can free us and end things now. Tell the police what you know about Dan."

Kyle sucked in a breath. "I dunno, Megs."

Luke's fingers brushed hers and she released the keys. He glanced at her out of the corner of his eye and nodded ever so slightly. She needed to keep Kyle distracted.

"How long have you been doing this?"

"Only a year. I didn't want to get involved, but I make next to nothing as a pharmacy technician and I have all this credit card debt, not to mention the house. The bank was breathing down my neck. I needed more income."

Kyle could justify it, but he was a drug dealer. People had overdosed on the drugs he sold them. He deserved to spend the rest of his life in jail.

She tamped down her anger and plastered an expression of sympathy on her face. "You were in a bad place. It couldn't have been an easy choice."

"It wasn't." He licked his lips. "I knew you would understand."

"I do. And that's why I'm looking out for you now. I care you about you, Kyle. Do you really think Dan does?"

"No, but he can't go against me either. I know too much." The hand holding the gun lowered to his side. He came around the coffee table, his expression earnest. "I'm sorry, Megs, but there's no other—"

Luke lunged from the couch and tackled Kyle. Both men went flying. They slammed into the bookcase, sending it crashing into the wall. Kyle's gun sailed through the air and landed on the carpet.

Megan rocked off the couch and kicked the weapon farther out of reach. The sound of glass crashing was followed by a grunt of pain. She turned. Luke was crumpled on the floor.

Kyle bolted for the door. He swung it open and ran for the garage. Luke struggled to his feet, grabbed his primary weapon from the wet bar, and checked to make sure it was loaded before cutting her loose.

"Take my backup," Luke ordered.

The gun was cool against her sweaty palm. Holding the weapon didn't erase the fear, but it put her on a more level playing field. She let out a breath. Luke scooped up his cell phone and dialed.

Shots rang out. Megan ducked behind the wet bar. It took her two heartbeats to realize they'd come from the garage.

"I need backup now," Luke said as he peeked over the counter. The roar of a truck's engine came from outside. "Suspects are escaping in a vehicle. A black truck. Names are Dan Carter and Kyle Franklin. They are armed and dangerous."

He paused as the vehicle passed outside the living room windows. "Correction. Only one suspect is in the vehicle. Chief Deputy Dan Carter."

Tires peeled, and Megan lifted her head high enough to see the truck speed down the driveway as Dan escaped.

The hospital emergency room was a hum of activity. Luke leaned against the wall, weariness seeping into his bones. He'd washed Kyle's blood off his hands, but it still stained his shirt and sports jacket. Dan had shot the younger man twice and left him for dead in the garage before fleeing.

Kyle was in surgery and his family was staked out in the waiting room. Sheriff Franklin's face was drawn and pale. He looked as if he'd aged a decade in only a few hours. Brent, dressed in his deputy uniform, paced the length of glass overlooking the parking lot. Cindy couldn't stop crying. Her nose was red and her eyes swollen.

Megan walked into the waiting room carrying two cups from the vending machine. Her hair was tangled, her shirt also stained with Kyle's blood, and a dark smudge of mascara marred one cheek. She handed one of the cups to Cindy, before taking a seat next to the other woman and fishing some fresh tissues out of her purse.

Luke couldn't hear her words, but he knew they were ones of comfort.

"Every cop in the state is looking for Dan," Weston said, drawing Luke's attention back to their conversation. "I'm sorry. We should've gotten there faster."

He snorted. "How? By teleportation. You were there within fifteen minutes of receiving the tip."

An individual had called the Medina County Sheriff's office and anonymously reported that Kyle was selling drugs taken from the evidence room. Weston had immediately tried to contact Luke to warn him and, not being able to find him, sent backup to Kyle's house. Unfortunately, Dan eluded the incoming troopers.

"Any idea where the tip came from?" Luke asked.

"We're trying to trace it now, but it came from a prepaid phone."

"Huh. The mysterious woman who called Megan also used a prepaid phone."

"Yeah, but our tip came from a man." Weston pulled out his cell phone and selected an audio file. He hit play, and the conversation between the dispatcher and the mysterious caller played out. When it finished, he asked, "Recognize the voice?"

"Something about the cadence is familiar, but he's using something to distort his voice, so I can't quite place it." Luke waved Brent and Sheriff Franklin over. "Play it again. Maybe they'll recognize it."

Weston did. Both men shook their heads.

Sheriff Franklin squeezed the bridge of his nose between

his thumb and forefinger. "This is a nightmare. Luke, I'm so sorry. I should've taken your concerns about Dan more seriously." He dropped his hand. "I trusted him because ten years ago, Dan saved my life while I was on vacation. His bravery earned my loyalty, and I never questioned it."

"I can see why." Luke turned to Brent. "I guess you knew about their history?"

Brent nodded. "I wanted to tell you, but it wasn't my place. It was the sheriff's story to share when and if he wanted."

Some of the pressure on Luke's shoulders lifted. He hadn't been able to understand why Brent and the sheriff were so protective of the chief deputy, but things were snapping into place.

"Dan took advantage of your loyalty," he said. "Neither of you have anything to feel bad about."

A doctor strolled into the emergency room. He wore scrubs and carried a face mask in his hand. "Franklin family?"

Cindy jumped from the chair. Brent and Sheriff Franklin flanked her. "Kyle's my brother."

Megan came next to Luke. He reached for her hand, sliding her fingers in between his.

"The surgery went well and your brother is resting now," the doctor said. "He was very lucky. Whoever provided first aid on the scene before the paramedics arrived likely saved his life. If he'd been left alone for another few minutes, I don't think we would've been able to save him."

Cindy burst into fresh tears and turned. She wrapped her arms around Luke first and then Megan.

"Thank you," she whispered. "Thank you. I know he's done horrible things, but he's..."

"He's your brother." Megan squeezed the other woman's arm. "And you love him."

The other members of the family shook their hands before they all moved away. Weston started to follow but paused. "Oh, hey, Luke. Before I forget, your dad stopped by the sheriff's department looking for you."

He rocked back on his heels. "He did? Did he say what he wanted?"

"Yeah. To make sure you were okay." Weston pointed to the television bolted to the ceiling. "You probably haven't been watching, but your face was all over the local news. He looked terrified. I didn't give him any information, but I did say you were unharmed. I hope that was okay."

"Yeah. Thanks."

Weston nodded. "Sure thing."

His colleague walked away, unaware of the impact his news had on Luke. His dad had gone to the sheriff's department to check on him? He wasn't sure what to do with that information. He'd broken his leg when he was six, had stitches at ten, and been hospitalized at thirteen after a car accident. His mother had called Patrick each time to let him know, but his father had never shown up to check on him. Not once.

Until today.

Lord, have I stubbornly refused to listen to You? Have You touched my dad's heart and changed him?

"Maybe you should call him." Megan squeezed his hand. "And if you need someone to hold your hand while you do…well, it seems I have dibs."

He tugged her closer, wrapping an arm around her waist. "You would do that?"

"I'm your friend. It's my job to hold you up."

Something inside Luke cracked. They'd nearly died today, and the entire time, all he could think about was that he hadn't told Megan the truth about his feelings. By the grace of God, he'd been given a second chance, and he wasn't going to squander it.

"Megs, I love you. I'm sorry I didn't say it the other night."

She sucked in a breath, her gaze scanning his face. "Why didn't you?"

"Because I was afraid we wouldn't be able to move past the mistakes and the hurt. There's a lot of history between us and it's not all good. I screwed up by keeping the truth of Wade's alcohol problem from you. I helped put him in prison. I know you said you've forgiven me, but that's not the same thing as reconciling and truly leaving the past in the past."

"Luke, you nearly died several times working this case. You're running down every lead and doing everything possible to prove Wade's innocence. Don't you think I see that?" She cupped his face in her hands. "You didn't just say you were sorry. You *showed* me you were."

His chest constricted so tightly, it was hard to draw in

215

a breath. There was nothing in the depths of her eyes except love.

"You weren't the only one who made mistakes," she continued. "I'd lost faith in everything. God, you, myself. But I was wrong. I should've stayed and fought, and I'm determined not to make the same mistake twice. I love you, Luke. And I'm in this for the long haul."

"I love you too, Megs."

He kissed her, his heart breaking free of the chains holding it down. She was his past. She was also his future. The good Lord hadn't just spared their lives, He'd given them a second chance. And Luke knew exactly how he felt in that moment with the love of his life in his arms.

Blessed.

TWENTY-ONE

Three days later, Luke stepped into the barn. The west side doors were open and a brilliant sunset painted the sky in hues of deep oranges and pale yellows. For a moment, he breathed in the air scented with horse and hay. Some of his exhaustion ebbed and his headache lessened.

This was his first time home for longer than a quick meal and a catnap since Dan's attack. The chief deputy was still at large. While the ranger team had gathered a lot of evidence against Dan, all of it related to stealing drugs and weapons from the evidence room. They hadn't found anything connecting him directly to Franny's murder.

"Megs?" Luke called out.

"I'm here."

He followed the sound of her voice around the corner and found her sitting on a hay bale, watching the sunset. She greeted him with a half smile. Dark circles shadowed the skin under her eyes, a testament to her own lack of sleep, and there was tension in the edges of her smile. Still, she stood and opened her arms, pushing up on her tiptoes to hug him.

Luke pulled back and kissed her gently. Megan's smile widened. The last rays of sunlight reflected off her hair, and he brushed a few strands out of her face.

He brushed her lips with his again. "Hey, you."

"Hey. Wanna pull up a hay bale and watch the sunset with me?"

"Absolutely."

They settled on the makeshift bench. He wrapped an arm around her waist, and Megan rested her head on his shoulder with a sigh.

"How did the interview with Kyle go?"

The sheriff's nephew had finally been well enough to question this afternoon, following a second surgery for his gunshot wounds.

"It was helpful in piecing together how Dan was stealing the evidence," Luke said. "Unfortunately, it didn't provide us with any new information on Franny's murder case. Kyle claims he had no idea Dan had anything to do with Franny's death until after you told him."

"I believe that. He looked shocked when he found out."

"What about you? Any new developments on your end?"

She nodded and picked at the hay bale. "We've

decided not to move forward with Wade's appeal at the moment."

"What?" He pulled back to look at her. "Why?"

"In order to get my brother out of jail, we have to file a writ of habeas corpus. The evidence we have so far isn't sufficient to invalidate Wade's confession and overturn his conviction. Dan didn't admit to killing Franny, and that makes a difference."

He rubbed a hand down her back. "I'm sorry."

It was unfair and a rotten hand. They'd torn Dan's house apart looking for evidence tying him to Franny's murder. Or Skeeter's. Or even Quentin's. But they'd come up empty on all fronts.

Even worse, Dan was out there somewhere. A danger to people in general, but a threat to Megan specifically. Luke understood the kind of man Dan was—vengeful and arrogant. He might be lying low now, but he would circle back around.

She twirled a piece a hay between her fingers. "I keep telling myself to have patience. It's only been a few days. I just want him out as soon as possible."

"I know you do. So do I."

Megan snuggled closer. "We'll reevaluate after all the evidence has been gone through and the audit at the sheriff's department is finished. Maybe my aunt will wake up and be able to help us. It's not the end of the road. It's just a speed bump. I'm going to keep praying and keep having faith."

"And working hard."

"Well, that's a given." She placed a kiss along the

bottom of his jaw. "How is the audit going? Has everyone else at the sheriff's department been officially cleared?"

"Not yet, but so far, so good. Sheriff Franklin has been top-notch. He's as determined to get justice for Franny, Skeeter, and Quentin as we are. Brent too. I think they feel terrible about putting so much faith in Dan. We've spent a lot of time talking the last couple of days, and as more has come out, they've realized what a master manipulator he was."

"There are so many loose ends to this case. I hate that." She rubbed her cheek. "I still think about the woman who called to warn me. I hope she's okay."

"Me too."

Luke had hoped she would come forward and reveal her identity now that Dan was exposed, but that hadn't happened.

"We haven't given up on finding her," he said. "There's a strong rodeo connection between Quentin, Franny, and Kyle. Maybe she's a part of that group."

"Chad was also involved in the rodeo."

"We interviewed him again yesterday. He brought his attorney, and they played hardball. He admitted to knowing all of these people, but I can't figure out his role in this. If there is one."

Her nose wrinkled. "Dan had to be covering some-thing up for him."

"That's my impression too. And the family, in general, was against our investigation. But Dan was focused on becoming the next sheriff. Maybe Chad did something illegal, something unrelated to Franny's murder, and Dan covered it up to get in the family's good graces."

"I could see that," Megan said. "He was stealing from the evidence room. It doesn't seem like a stretch to believe he would cover up someone else's crime. Makes you wonder how many others he's done that for."

"Well, along with auditing the evidence room, we're going to look at every single one of Dan's cases for that very reason. It'll take a long time to go through everything, but I don't want anything overlooked. I also don't think we're at the end of this drug ring either. Kyle doesn't know much, but he's lower level."

Just another reason why they needed to get their hands on Dan. It was like the man had disappeared into thin air. No one had seen his truck or him. Frustration nipped at Luke and he took a deep breath.

Lord, I know You have Your own timing, but finding some clue as to Dan's whereabouts would be really helpful.

They sat in silence for a while, each lost in their own thoughts, as the sun sank behind the trees.

"Have you talked to your dad?" Megan asked.

"Not since we had lunch the other day."

It'd been brief, since Luke was in the middle of a massive investigation, but long overdue. Patrick had given a heartfelt apology, and Luke had sorely underestimated the healing it would offer.

"Maybe when things settle down, we can all get together."

"I'd like that." She stood from the hay bale and

stretched. "Goodness, I'm getting old. When I was a kid, I could sit on those forever. Did I ever tell you my dad built a special spot for me in the hayloft of our barn?"

"No. I knew you liked to hang in the barn and think, but I never knew why."

"It was quiet. Wade had colic when he was a baby and a very healthy set of lungs." She swiped the hay off the back of her jeans. "I used to hang out in the barn to get away from the house. My daddy noticed, and he set up this special place for me in the hayloft. I used to go up there and read or write in my diary. I even had—"

She froze and her eyes widened.

"What is it?" Luke looked behind him, but no one was there.

Megan yanked on the chain around her neck and pulled out the key attached. Her fingers closed around it.

"I think I know what this goes to."

It only took five minutes to travel the distance between Luke's property and June's, but Megan's mind raced the entire way.

"I can't believe I never thought of it," she said, silently urging Luke to put more pressure on the gas pedal. "June knew I was struggling after my parents' death, and she built me a similar hangout space in her hayloft. It's so simple and obvious."

"How long has it been since you used the loft?"

"Not since freshman year in high school. Life got too

busy after that, but when I was younger, I would hide things in the rafters to prevent Wade from finding them."

Luke pulled into June's driveway and shoved the vehicle into park. "What makes you think June would've done the same?"

"Because she specifically told Quentin's family to stay quiet about her investigation." Megan clambered out of the truck. "My aunt knew this investigation was dangerous. Her office was inside her house, and June was smart enough to figure out Dan would've done anything to silence her and destroy her notes."

Lights flashed behind them as Sheriff Franklin drove up. Megan had a moment's hesitation when they'd called him, but Franny's murder was still within his jurisdiction and he'd been cleared by the ranger team.

"Thanks for coming so quickly, Sheriff," Luke said.

"You caught me at a good time." He huddled farther down into his coat as a wind rustled the leaves. "I was on my way home."

Megan flipped on her cell phone's light to guide her way across the yard. Luke fell into step beside her, carrying a heavy-duty flashlight. The sheriff's portable radio crackled, and dispatch said something Megan couldn't make out. Sheriff Franklin answered before running to catch up.

The barn door creaked open. Megan didn't bother with the light switch. Power had been turned off to the property after the fire. She quickly climbed the stairs to the hayloft, the men following behind. Luckily, it was well built and big enough for all of them.

Sheriff Franklin ducked to prevent knocking his head against the ceiling. "Okay, what are we looking for?"

Megan turned in a circle, shining her light on the ceiling. "Anything tucked inside the rafters. I'm not sure what June would've put up here, but my guess is, we'll need a key to open it."

Luke's flashlight was much better, and he swept it across the wooden beams. Something metallic caught Megan's eye in the far rear corner. A pile of hay blocked the way.

She pointed. "There."

Sheriff Franklin pulled a camera out of his pocket. "Shine your flashlight over there, Luke."

Megan bounced on the balls of her feet as the lawmen went through the procedures necessary to preserve the evidence. It took everything in her not to scream at them to hurry. Finally, Luke handed his flashlight to the sheriff and climbed up on the hay bales.

"What is it?" she asked.

"It's a portable safe."

Luke grunted and pulled, nearly knocking himself off his perch in the process, but finally made it down with the safe. He set it on the ground, and Megan shoved her phone in her jacket pocket. Her fingers trembled as she unclasped the chain around her neck.

The sheriff continued to take pictures. Megan sucked in a deep breath and glanced at Luke. He nodded. She stuck the key in the lock and turned.

The safe clicked opened. *Thank you, Lord.*

Her heart thundered. She pulled back the lid. Inside

were several file folders, labeled in her aunt's neat hand, but it was the edges of a moleskin journal that caught Megan's eye. She pulled it out and opened it. Unfamiliar scrawls lined the pages.

The sheriff's edged closer. "That's Franny's handwriting."

"It's her journal."

Megan ran her finger down the page, scanning it. Nothing on the page was about Dan. Franny was complaining about her dad and how she was determined to get answers for what he'd done. She was angry with him, although Megan couldn't figure out why.

Luke had already removed a file folder and opened it.

"Megs, these are copies of your aunt's investigation notes. There are also copies of official reports, including the ones that went missing." He flashed the page so she could see it, although it was too dark to make out more than the Medina County Sheriff Department logo at the top. "Here's Chad's original interview."

"Hold on, guys." Sheriff Franklin held up his hands. "We all want to go through this box, but we should do it back at the department, not in the middle of a hay loft."

"He's right." Luke frowned and closed the file folder. "I should call Lieutenant Rodriguez and inform her as well. She may want Weston to join us."

With reluctance, Megan set the journal back inside the safe. How had her aunt gotten her hands on it? And what was in those pages, in Franny's thoughts, that could help their case?

Luke closed the lid but didn't bother locking it. "Let's go."

Within minutes, the safe was loaded between the front seats of Luke's vehicle and they were on the road. The sheriff led the way in his own patrol car.

"This changes everything." Megan's leg jittered against the seat. "Right?"

"It definitely gives us a new angle." He reached out and took her head. "Great job, Megs. We wouldn't have found it without you."

"Not until June woke up anyway—What's wrong?"

"Looks like the sheriff is having car trouble." Luke stopped behind the patrol truck. The country road was dark and empty, so neither man bothered to pull off to the side. "Hold on a sec."

Luke hopped out, joined the sheriff, and together the two men popped open the hood. She couldn't hear their words, only a few muffled murmurs. Megan's phone rang. Grace's name flashed on screen.

She answered without saying hello. "Did you get my text? Isn't it amazing—"

"Megs, listen." Her friend's tone was sharp. "I don't think Dan was working alone—"

A gunshot rang out.

Sheriff Franklin fell against his patrol truck before crumpling to the ground. Someone screamed. Luke dove for the ground, disappearing from view.

Glass shattered as more bullets flew. Megan undid her seat belt and ducked into the wheel well. Someone was still screaming, and it took her three rapid heartbeats to realize it was her. She snapped her mouth shut.

"Megan! Megan!"

Grace's voice came from far away. The passenger side door opened as bullets pelted the Suburban. Luke shoved her head down farther, his fingers tangling in her hair. The windshield shattered, raining squares of glass down on top of them.

Silence. It was eerily loud in the wake of the gunshots. Megan was dizzy.

"Breathe, babe," Luke commanded. "Breathe."

She sucked in a gulp of air. Her heart was hammering like a jackrabbit. Luke pulled her from the wheel well. "You hit?"

Megan ran a hand over her chest. "No. You?"

"No."

He yanked his backup weapon from his boot and handed it to her, before reaching in the vehicle and unlatching his rifle. His radio crackled and dispatch directed backup to respond to their exact location.

God bless, Grace. She'd alerted authorities—probably by calling Weston—and they'd used the GPS locator in Luke's state vehicle to find them. Still, judging from the rapid chat on the radio, it would take a while for backup to arrive.

"He must want what's in the safe." Luke scanned the tree line on the other side of the Suburban. "The shooter put himself high to get a line of sight, but now he's coming to check if we're dead."

227

Her hands trembled. She sucked in another breath. "Franny's journal. He has to be after the journal."

Luke reached inside the vehicle and fished it out of the safe. He handed it to her.

"Take cover in the woods before he gets here and don't look back. Don't wait for me." He kissed her hard. "No matter what you hear, no matter what happens, run."

She hugged the journal to her chest. "What about you?"

"The sheriff is wounded. I can't leave him unprotected." He lifted his rifle. "Now go!"

There was no time for arguments, no chance for debate. He didn't give it to her. Luke pushed her toward the trees. Megan darted across the asphalt, the canopy of safety too far away. Shots rang out. Something whizzed past her ear and she nearly screamed.

Run. Run. Run.

She burst across the tree line and tripped over a root. She stumbled and caught herself on a nearby pine. Bark scraped the skin on the outer edge of her hand. The rush of her heartbeat mingled with the sharp intake of her own breath.

She turned back to the road. Luke lay in the middle of the asphalt, a dark stain spreading underneath him. Megan lunged toward him. Bile rose in the back of her throat.

No, Lord, no. Not Luke. Please, God, we've just found each other again.

A shadowy figure stepped from the opposite tree line,

a rifle held ready. Megan ducked. The tree next to her head exploded, spraying bark and shards of wood.

She spun on her heel and took off. If the shooter wanted Franny's journal, then he could come and take it. Distracting him would give backup time to arrive and help Luke and Sheriff Franklin.

The trees flew past. The scent of leaves and dirt and her own fear choked her. She tripped over another root and slammed to the ground. Luke's gun sailed out of her hand, landing in the bushes. She crawled over, her hands patting the earth while desperate seconds ticked by.

A rustle came from the leaves. Megan bolted to her feet, leaving the gun behind, and ran. The trees thinned. A lake shimmered in the moonlight. The house Franny had been killed in wasn't far.

Her legs trembling and her lungs burning, Megan was forced to slow down. How had the shooter figured out they'd found the journal?

Don't trust anyone.

Her aunt's voice mail held a warning she needed to heed. Chest heaving, Megan's gaze darted around, and she spotted a fallen branch covered in bushes. Slipping her hands between the branches, she shoved Franny's journal underneath the log. She wasn't taking any chances.

Deed done, she raced along the edge of the tree line around the lake. The roads intersected on the west side. If she could get there, she could find help. She willed more power into her legs.

A figure darted out from the bushes and blocked her

path. She gasped and drew up short, skidding against the wet pine needles and nearly falling backward. Dressed in camouflage and boots, night-vision goggles hung round his neck, Heath Dickerson pointed a rifle straight at Megan's heart.

TWENTY-TWO

"Give me the journal," Heath demanded.

Megan heart thundered against her ribcage. She backed up a step.

"Don't move," he barked. "And don't even think about lying. I know you retrieved it from June's barn. I have a police scanner and heard every word Sheriff Franklin said to dispatch."

She swallowed. "I don't have it."

"It wasn't in Luke's truck, so I'll ask one more time before I shoot." His tone was hard. "Where. Is. The. Journal?"

Think. Think. She pulled air into her lungs. "I hid it."

He glared at her for a long heartbeat. "Unzip your jacket."

She did, opening it wide so he could see the journal wasn't tucked inside. She lifted it and turned around.

He rushed her, wrapped a hand around her throat,

and shoved her against a tree. "I ought to choke the living daylights out of you."

A branch dug into the back of her head. Heat rose in her body as Heath squeezed tighter. Megan couldn't breathe. She grasped his hand in a futile attempt to break his hold. Her lungs burned and her vision blurred.

He released her and she tumbled to the ground. She wheezed.

"Get up. Show me where you hid the journal." He bent down, his hot breath whispering along her cheek. "I can make your death easy, or painful. The choice is yours."

Megan drew in shallow breaths. Sharp pain stabbed her lungs. "Okay. I'll take you."

She used the tree as support and staggered to her feet. Like a drunk, she weaved. Megan closed her eyes, willing her body to cooperate. She'd bought time, and every second meant hope.

Luke had taught her that.

Tears pricked her eyes, and she battled them back. She couldn't think about Luke or she would lose it. She needed to focus. Slipping her hand into her jacket pocket, Megan unlocked her phone. Blindly, using only muscle memory, she hit the call button. If luck was with her, Grace would answer and record the conversation.

"Why do you want the journal?" Megan moved the speaker of her phone outward, praying it would pick up their words.

He laughed. "Your last minutes on earth and that's what you want to discuss."

"If I'm going to die, I might as well know why." She needed to get his confession, and the best way was to appeal to his ego. "Your plan was brilliant. You've kept us running in circles."

Heath chuckled, a smirk playing on his lips. "I did have ya'll chasing your tails, didn't I?"

Megan let out the breath she was holding. Her hunch was right. At his core, Heath was a show-off and desperate for a chance to brag about his accomplishments.

"So, go on and tell me. Franny figured out you were working with Dan to steal from the evidence room, didn't she?"

Heath's expression hardened. "She betrayed me. Sticking her nose where it didn't belong. Sheriff Franklin promised me she would only work on the historical cases. He was wrong."

"When did she figure out you were involved?"

"Two weeks before her death, she caught me in the evidence room. I gave her an excuse, but I could tell she wasn't buying it."

Based on evidence the rangers found, a small dig into the records would've revealed things were missing from the evidence room. Franny had deduced her father was working with people in the sheriff's department, and she'd tried to figure out who. It was a brave move for the young woman to take and she'd paid with her life.

"It was smart to team up with Dan," Megan said, appealing again to his ego. "How did you two start working together?"

"I needed fast cash. Dan wanted to be the next sheriff, and I had the influence to make that happen. It was a win-win." He shoved the rifle muzzle into her back. "Walk faster."

She picked up her pace half a beat. "Did you hire Quentin, or was that Dan?"

"Me. I knew Quentin from the rodeo days. We stored the guns and drugs we took from the evidence room on my ranch, and he picked them up for sale."

"Things must have been going well for you until Quentin figured out you'd given the okay for Dan to kill your daughter."

Megan was taking a guess, but it was an educated one. The chief deputy wouldn't have murdered Franny without Heath's permission.

"They were going well." His jaw clenched. "My daughter should've stayed out of it. I warned her, but she wouldn't listen."

Bile churned in Megan's stomach. Franny had been killed by Dan, but she'd been betrayed by her own father.

"Quentin kept the gun and tried to use it against you to get out of the business." She adjusted her grip on the phone in her pocket. "But you didn't let him, did you?"

"Nope." His expression twisted, becoming sinister and cruel. "I tied him up and gave him a dose of barbiturates. No one—absolutely no one—threatens me."

"Quentin should have known better."

She swallowed hard, struggling with another wave of nausea. Health's callousness was disgusting.

"Turning on you was disloyal," she added for good measure.

He nodded. "Exactly. After all I'd done for him. He deserved what was coming to him."

Megan pushed a branch out of the way. How far was the road? How far away was backup? She needed to keep him talking.

"Who came up with the idea to frame Wade for Franny's death?"

"Dan. Franny was getting close to figuring out who I was working with, but she hadn't quite made it. She was focused on Brent and Sheriff Franklin. Dan stole Wade's phone during the party. Afterward, he stopped by Franny's house under the guise of neighbor complaints regarding loud music. He helped her clean up and found Wade's phone in the cushions where he'd hidden it earlier in the evening. Franny called Wade, and before he got there Dan killed her. It was the perfect setup."

A shudder ran down her spine. He was discussing his daughter's murder as if he was organizing a Sunday picnic.

"Afterward, the whole thing with Quentin happened, and I decided the risk of exposure was too great," he continued. "I told Dan to recruit Kyle."

That explained why Kyle had no idea Heath was involved.

"Wasn't it risky to recruit the sheriff's nephew?"

"Naw. I knew from the rodeo days Kyle had a tendency to walk on the wrong side of the line. Besides, we never sold any drugs or weapons inside Medina

County. We always sold them in other areas to prevent the sheriff from catching on." He glared at her. "We were supposed to expand our operation once Dan was sheriff by manufacturing meth and shipping in other drugs. Between his control of the department and my political connections, we were set to be unstoppable."

The corruption would've spread like a cancer, infiltrating every corner of the county and moving throughout the state. Megan's stomach twisted at the thought. Still, she had to keep stroking his ego.

"You still can, I'm sure. The steps you took to protect yourself were perfect. No one thinks you're a part of this."

He nodded. "I made sure of it."

"What about Skeeter?" she asked.

"That..." Heath growled. "That piece of trash deserved what he got. I couldn't stand seeing him around town knowing he'd tried to separate my daughter from her family. He disrespected me."

He was insane. His logic was off the wall. Megan mentally calculated how long she could hold up this charade. She had the feeling time was running out.

Lord, give me strength.

Her gaze shot to the weapon in Heath's hands. "Is that the rifle you used to shot Skeeter?"

"No, I had to get rid of it, which really ticked me off. That rifle was my trophy. Every time I looked at it, I remembered shooting Skeeter. It was supposed to take out you and Luke too."

Except he missed. It wasn't wise to mention that mistake.

Megan licked her dry lips. "We played right into your hands by taking the saddles from the tack room. Spray-painting the message on the wall was a nice touch. But who was responsible for the fire? And June's car accident?" Her steps faltered. "The attack on Wade in prison?"

"All me. Dan helped me coordinate them, but after the shooting in the woods, I knew it was only a matter of time before you linked it to Skeeter's death. The plan was to frame Kyle and Sheriff Franklin for the thefts and the murders. That way we could speed up our takeover of the sheriff's department." He shoved her again with the muzzle. "Where is the journal?"

"Just a little further."

Please God, I know You are with me. Help me think of a way to keep him talking, give me the right words.

She chewed on the inside of her cheek. "You were the anonymous caller. The one who called the sheriff's department to report Kyle."

A smile stretched across Heath's face. "Someone had to take the fall. Dan was supposed to drop off a huge shipment at Kyle's house for law enforcement to find and then leave."

Except Luke and Megan had arrived unexpectedly to interview Kyle, throwing the plan off.

"That was smart to set up Kyle." She paused. "How could you be sure he wouldn't flip on you?"

"Dan had already convinced Kyle he would get him

out of any trouble if he was ever arrested." Heath puffed out his cheeks. "But the truth is we planned to kill him after he was arrested. County jail can be a dangerous place you know. Of course, all of that went out the window when Dan was caught at Kyle's."

He scanned the woods and then glared at her. Heath's patience was wearing thin. She had to stall him, but change tactics.

"The journal is near here."

Megan stopped and glanced around as if looking for her spot. Her mind whirled, trying to think of a way to distract him and buy more time.

"Since Dan knows about the operation, he's a liability. Surely you have a plan to take care of things."

"You'd be right." He chuckled. "The dummy ran straight for my house after he escaped. Dan's tied up in a barn on the far edge of my property. Once I'm done with you, I'll kill him. It'll be framed like a suicide, of course." He patted the rifle again. "This baby will be in his truck with him and the entire case will be neatly tied up."

Megan's skin crawled. He was twisted and sick. She parted some leaves on a bush, as if she was looking for the journal.

"And then?"

"Well, I've shot Sheriff Franklin. I'll put out feelers for another sheriff, one who can be bought to look the other way. The rest of the plan will remain the same." He chuckled again. "Once I eliminate you, I have a syringe full of barbiturates with June's name on it. Everyone who is a threat to me will be gone."

Heat rose in Megan, and her hands tightened on the branches. He wasn't getting anywhere near her family as long as she had breath in her body. There had to be a way to stop him.

"How did June get Franny's journal?"

"My stupid cow of a wife." Health's mouth hardened and his eyes narrowed. "She thought she could turn on me. Karen was meeting with June at the mall in Woodville periodically. I installed spy software on my wife's phone a long time ago. Amazing stuff. You can turn the phone into a listening device and I overheard their conversations. The last time they met, June convinced her tell Luke everything."

"You put steering fluid in the brake line so my aunt would have a car accident while she was meeting with Karen."

"Yep. I wanted to kill my wife too, but I couldn't afford the attention." He formed a fist and shook it. "I taught her a lesson, though."

The implication was clear. He'd beaten Karen and terrorized her into silence. He'd probably been doing it for years. When Karan had gotten a glimpse of freedom, a helping hand from June, Heath had taken it away.

"After June's accident, I locked Karen in the house," Heath continued.

Yet, she'd used a prepaid phone to warn Megan. Did Heath know? It was possible he'd found out afterward. Karen had only called once. Megan winced thinking that Franny's mother had been beaten for helping.

"Enough playing around. You've examined every

bush in this area." Heath raised the rifle. "Where's the journal?"

She licked her lips, her gaze darting into the woods.

"You're screwing with me, aren't you?" he snapped. "You have no idea where it is."

Could she make a run for it? It was the only option she had left. Megan edged toward some thick under-brush. "I..."

"Don't even think about it. You won't make it ten feet." Heath grinned. "I'm a hunter after all. Nice knowing you, Megan."

A shadow flew out of the trees and tackled Heath with a fierce roar. The two shapes rolled across the dirt and crashed into a tree. A familiar voice let out a grunt.

Luke!

Thank you, God.

The slap of flesh hitting flesh accompanied another roll across the forest floor. Heath's rifle was spit out of the fight and Megan dove for the weapon. She wouldn't leave Luke to battle alone.

Her hand closed over the metal. She hauled it to her shoulder, thankful for the shooting lessons from her aunt, and placed her finger next to the trigger.

"Stop," she commanded.

The men paid her no heed. Heath landed a punch hard enough to snap Luke's head back. They went rolling again, a blur of fabric and fists. Megan couldn't shoot Heath without fear of hitting Luke.

With a guttural growl and one swift movement, Luke

whipped a knife out of his boot, straddled Heath, and held the blade to his throat. The other man froze.

Megan let out the breath she was holding and edged closer. Dark liquid coated the side of Luke's face and stained his shirt.

Blood. It was blood.

"I'm covering you, Luke." Her voice trembled. "Cuff him."

He slapped the cuffs on Health, before hauling the criminal to his feet.

Luke lifted the knife in his hand. The pearl handle glimmered in the moonlight. "June's gift saves the day again."

Flashlights flickered and men called out.

"Here," Megan cried, putting the rifle on the ground. "We're here."

Half a dozen troopers swarmed. One took Heath from Luke and another collected the rifle.

Megan ran to Luke. She gripped his chin and turned his head. Blood was caked to his hair.

"How bad is it?"

"I'm okay, Megs." He gently grasped her wrist. "The bullet nicked me. I passed out for a couple of minutes, but I'm fine. There's a lot of blood because head wounds do that."

He was there. Solid muscle and warm skin. Alive. Her body shook as silent sobs racked her, so deep she couldn't catch her breath.

Luke's expression went from concern to full-blown

terror. His hands traced the line of her back, his gaze scanning over her.

"Are you okay? Are you hurt?"

"N-n-n-noooo." She sucked in a shuddering breath. "I saw you lying on the ground with all that blood around you and... I thought..." She gripped his shoulders. "I warned you. You're not bulletproof."

"Oh, babe." Luke gathered her against him, rocking her, his hands running through her hair. "It'll take more than a lunatic with a rifle to separate me from you."

She raised her face to look at him, tears dripping off her chin. "I don't want to be without you."

His eyes shimmered with unshed tears. "You won't, Megs. You won't."

TWENTY-THREE

Nine months later

In a few minutes, the first guests would arrive for her aunt's housewarming party, and Megan wanted everything perfect. She straightened the picture frame and backed up to examine her work.

"A little to the left," Wade remarked, pausing as he poured ice into a giant cooler. His eyes twinkled with amusement.

"Stop trying to trick me." She swatted his arm. "And hurry up with that ice. You're going to drip water all over the floor."

Megan turned away, and a cold rush swept down her back. She screeched and jumped, pulling at her T-shirt. An ice cube clattered to the floor.

She spun on her heel. Wade was already backing up

across the kitchen, his hands raised in surrender, but his shoulders shook with laughter.

"I'm sooooo gonna get you back for that," she declared, stalking him, her own chuckles bubbling up. She grabbed a piece of ice from the bag.

June strolled into the room, her yellow dress fluttering around her legs. Her hair was styled and light makeup accented the flecks of blue in her eyes.

"Protect me, Aunt June."

Wade leaped behind his aunt and used her as a shield. It only increased Megan's laughter. Her brother towered over the older woman by three heads.

Megan raised her ice cube. "Come here and take it like a man."

"Stop that, both of you." June scowled, although it held no heat. Her lips twitched. "You're acting like a pair of six-year-olds. And Megan, if you get water on me and ruin my hairstyle, I'll be furious."

Wade's grin broadened, and he did a victory dance. Megan dumped her ice cube in the sink and, once her aunt had moved out of the way, sprayed cold flecks of water in her brother's face. He scooped her up for a bear hug and she squealed again.

The doorbell rang.

"Put me down, you oaf, and finish putting the ice in the lemonade." Megan kissed her brother's cheek before he released her. "I'll get the door. It's probably Luke."

"Thank goodness. I can't wait for him to fire up the grill. I'm starving."

Megan half ran to the door. She paused when the

light reflected off her engagement ring and took a heart-beat to admire it. Luke had reset the original solitaire diamond in a new setting, and it was the perfect representation of their relationship. A foundation of friendship and love refreshed into something stronger and even more beautiful.

She turned the handle and swung open the door. Nancy and Hank greeted her with broad smiles.

"Come in, come in." She stepped back. "Hank, would you like any help with those?"

"No, darlin', I've got it." He adjusted the grocery sacks in his hand. "Just point me in the way of the kitchen."

"Go on straight back. It's where the old one used to be."

In the redesign and rebuilding of June's house, she'd kept most of the old floor plan. There were some major improvements, like a spacious living room and an up-to-date office, but it retained the cozy quality that made it home.

Megan turned in time to see Luke strolling up the walkway. He was handsome in his cowboy hat and boots. She ran down the porch steps to greet him, and he caught her in his arms. Her heart soared as their lips met.

"Hello, wife." Luke brushed his lips against hers again. "I missed you."

"I missed you too."

He'd been working for the past week on a serious case in a nearby county. It was the first separation since their wedding and honeymoon two months ago, but it wouldn't be the last. Luke's job as a Texas Ranger occasionally called him away, but his work was important and Megan was happy to support him.

"This place looks amazing." Luke's gaze drifted over the front porch and the flowerbed filled with sunflowers. "I love what you've done with the landscaping."

"Wait till you see the inside."

She tugged on his hand. Nancy already had a glass of pink lemonade and was getting a grand tour from June. Hank and Wade trailed behind the women.

"Gorgeous." Nancy craned her head, taking in the high ceilings. "Every room is stunning."

"Wade had a big hand in it." Megan's chest swelled with pride. "He was here every day, working alongside the contractors, to ensure the house was built to June's specifications."

"I couldn't have asked for a better foreman," June said, wrapping her arm around Wade's waist.

He beamed. "Construction suits me. I've got another project starting up next week."

Megan said a silent prayer of thanksgiving. Having her family together, and happy, brought her constant joy.

The oven buzzer rang and June grabbed a pot holder. "That must be my quiche."

Luke leaned over and whispered, "Your aunt made a quiche?"

She bit her lip to keep from laughing. "It's your mother's fault. She read all those cookbooks and talked about recipes while June was in the coma. It seems to have rubbed off."

The two women had their heads together, staring down at the quiche and talking. Wade and Hank disappeared to grab some extra chairs from the back of his truck.

"Want to take a quick walk with me before everyone arrives?" Megan asked. Her stomach was jittery and her hands went clammy. She let out a breath and willed herself to act normal. "The quick phone calls we've had the past week haven't been enough."

"I know. Let's go."

They ducked out the back door. The air was warm and balmy, the lingering rays of sunlight casting pretty shadows through the trees. In the distance, Cinnamon grazed. Luke took her hand, interlocking their fingers together, as they strolled across the yard.

"How's your case going?" he asked. "Any progress?"

"Some." Megan had kept her law partnership with Grace and expanded by opening a second office in Cardin. Business was better than ever. "How about you?"

"Caught the bad guys." He grinned. "That makes for a good day. I stopped at the post office to pick up our mail and ran into Brent. He sends his regards."

"How does he like being the chief deputy?"

"It suits him. Sheriff Franklin was smart to extend the position. I suspect he's only delayed his retirement long enough to prepare Brent to take his place."

Thanks to his bullet proof vest, Sheriff Franklin had survived being shot by Heath. He'd stayed on as sheriff and, along with the state police, cleared his department of corruption. Dan, Heath, and Kyle were all sentenced to prison, although Kyle received a lighter sentence for cooperating with the district attorney.

"Hey, I don't know if I told you, but my dad is coming tonight," Luke said.

Over the last eight months, Luke and his father had built a fledgling relationship. Time, Patrick's sobriety, and a lot of prayer had gone a long way to healing their wounds.

"That's great." She kept her pace easy, even though all she wanted to do was sprint across the yard to the hay bales leaning against the barn. "Karen Dickerson is coming tonight too. She and June have become really good friends. Karen's even joined the Bible study group on Wednesdays."

"Things have been very different for her since Heath went to jail and Chad completed rehab. She looks happy every time I see her in town." Luke kissed the back of Megan's hand, and his mouth turned down. "Are you okay? You seem...a bit nervous."

"I'm fine."

She was trying for breezy, but the words came out strangled. How was it possible she could argue cases in front of some of the toughest judges in Texas, but when it came to Luke she couldn't keep her head?

They reached the fence line. In front of them was a gorgeous sunset and Megan sighed. "I don't think there's anything prettier."

Luke tugged her closer, his gaze on her and not the sky. "You got that right."

Her lips turned up. "You're a sweet-talker, Luke Tatum."

"Only when it comes to you, Megs."

She was tempted to kiss him, but her heart was already racing from nerves. Megan held up a finger. "Hold on."

She raced to the nearby hay bale and searched for the present she'd hidden there earlier. The jelly bean wrapping paper stuck out, making it easy to find.

She gave to Luke with a broad grin. "Happy two-month anniversary."

"Ah, babe." He groaned. "I didn't get you anything."

"You came straight from work. Besides, I don't need you to get me anything." She bounced on the balls of her feet and clapped her hands. "Now, open it."

He tore the wrapping paper, lifted the lid on the box, and laughed. Luke pulled out a bag of jelly beans. "Is this a present for me or for you?"

"That's for both of us."

She took it from him and ripped it open, popping a couple in her mouth. He snagged a red one from the bag, chuckling.

Megan pointed to the box. "There's more."

He glanced down and all mirth fled his expression. His mouth dropped open, and he looked at her, eyes wide. Luke blinked.

"Is this...is this..."

"It's the first outfit." Megan pressed her lips together and pulled the cloth out of the box. It was a white baby onesie etched with the words, Mommy and Daddy's

Little Jelly Bean. She placed it over her belly. "I'm pregnant."

Luke let out a whoop that could be heard for miles. He picked her up and swung her around in his arms, making her giggle. Jelly beans spilled from the bag, dusting the grass with their bright colors.

He set her down and cupped her face. "You've made me a very happy man, Megs. I love you."

Tears sparkled in his eyes, and she felt her own well up.

"I love you too."

Made in the USA
Middletown, DE
22 July 2019